"Will you come with me to Venice?" he asked. "It is so m... Paris. We could ride together in a gondola, and the bridges and palaces would glide past our heads while the gondolier sang us a love song. Does that not sound better than sitting around on a farm with Toni and her boyfriend?"

"Yes," I said, sighing. "It sounds much better. But I have a boyfriend at home, and I'm just in Europe to keep an eye on Toni. I'm going to see the Louvre and the French countryside and go home with my heart in one piece."

He looked at me seriously and nodded. "If that's what you want, Jill, then I must say goodbye. I hope you have a wonderful life." His hand brushed mine in a quick caress, then he turned and hurried away.

I got back to the hotel in a daze. *I'm glad that's the way it ended*, I kept telling myself. *I'm glad I didn't let him kiss me. But if everything has turned out so right, why do I feel like crying?*

Bantam Sweet Dreams Romances by Janet Quin-Harkin
Ask your bookseller for the books you have missed

The Great Boy Chase

Janet Quin-Harkin

BANTAM BOOKS
TORONTO · NEW YORK · LONDON · SYDNEY · AUCKLAND

RL 6, IL age 11 and up

THE GREAT BOY CHASE
A Bantam Book / September 1985

Cover photo by Pat Hill

ISBN 0-553-25071-X

Published simultaneously in the United States and Canada

*Bantam Books are published by Bantam Books, Inc. Its trademark,
consisting of the words ''Bantam Books'' and the portrayal of
a rooster, is Registered in U.S. Patent and Trademark Office
and in other countries. Marca Registrada. Bantam Books, Inc.,
666 Fifth Avenue, New York, New York 10103.*

PRINTED IN THE UNITED STATES OF AMERICA

O   0 9 8 7 6 5 4 3 2 1

The Great Boy Chase

Chapter One

My name is Jill Gardner, and my best friend is Toni Redmond. Anyone who knows us, knows that I'm not the sort of person who would chase a boy halfway around the world. Toni is that sort of person. She's the one who's always wild and impractical: I'm the sensible one. I try to reason her out of one crazy scheme after another, only to find myself right in the middle of some insane situation.

Anyone who doesn't know us would never believe that Toni is the leader of us both. She's pint-sized, wide-eyed, and helpless looking. I am tall, sleek-haired, and elegant. Toni has been leading me into a string of troubles since second grade—including, but not ending with, our senior year in high school.

Our last year in school things changed a lot. I think we both grew up. Some of it probably had to do with what happened during the summer before senior year. We had dated college guys and had summer jobs. But whatever it was, I know that during my senior year I felt much more mature and self-confident. In fact, I miraculously turned into one of those girls who had swept past me in the halls looking as if she owned the building. But I tried never to act like a snob the way they had done because I remembered what it felt like to be a little, scared freshman!

Toni had also matured miraculously. She started working hard to get good grades, which gave her less time for wild schemes. She made the girls' soccer team—having three older brothers and a lethal kick helped there—and she got the lead in the musical we did in May.

I went with Craig my whole senior year. He was kind, considerate, and fun, and it didn't hurt my image one bit to be seen with a super-good-looking college guy! Toni had also acquired a really great boyfriend, Rich. He'd been her biology partner and rescued her after she'd almost fainted when a worm landed on her knee. From that day on, he cut up all of the frogs and worms for her. Toni obviously enjoyed his protectiveness, despite her self-sufficiency in most things. He was quiet and serious and had helped Toni scrape into college.

I was sitting up in my room one June afternoon, going over the last few months in my mind and thinking about how we had changed. My graduation roses still stood in their glass vase on my vanity—wilted now and red-brown, but much too precious to throw away. My prom corsage, equally withered and turning brown, hung from my mirror. My invitation to Awards Night, my two certificates of commendation, and the program from the school musical were tucked into the mirror as well. All of them were already memories of my last school days.

I couldn't believe it was over. It seemed like only a short time before that I'd held my mother's hand and been dragged into kindergarten. And now I was a college-student-to-be. So why did I feel that little twinge of fear as I looked back at the reminders of school? All we had done for four years was count the days until we got out. I was out now. Assignment high school complete. Future planned. Nothing to worry about ever again. A whole summer ahead of me for relaxing and working part-time in the same day camp as the year before. I'd see Craig in the evenings and on weekends, and double-date with Toni and Rich—if she got back together with him.

I forgot to mention that after behaving like a mature, normal person for most of the school year, Toni blew it the last couple of months of school. It was getting the lead in the musical that did it. I don't mean that stardom went to her head. I mean that her leading man was a French exchange student, Philippe Moreau. We were doing *South Pacific,* and she played the American nurse, and he played the French planter. They were both perfect for their roles. So perfect, in fact, that they fell madly in love.

At the beginning, Toni did nothing but complain about Philippe. "He's a pain," she used to say. "He's so good-looking that he expects every girl to worship him. Well, he's sadly mistaken about this girl."

But then they started rehearsing the romantic scenes, and suddenly it was Romance with a capital *R.* They walked around together all day, holding hands, gazing into each other's eyes. It was sickening to watch. I didn't like Philippe too much. There was something about the conceited way that he smiled, as if he thought the whole world was watching and admiring him. Anyway, I was glad he was going back to France, safely far away. Now Toni could go back to Rich again, and everything would be just fine.

Oh, there would be dramatic scenes for a while. Toni was a great one for dramatic scenes. Heaven knew what she'd be like when she returned from the "Great Farewell" at the airport.

I glanced at my watch. At that very minute Philippe would be embracing her for the last time. He'd walk bravely toward the plane while Toni yelled, loud enough for the whole airport to hear, that she'd always love him. I smiled to myself as I imagined the scene. I had offered to go with her to the airport, but she'd refused. She didn't like anyone to see her cry. She'd always been tough. I don't ever remember seeing her cry even in the second grade. So I didn't expect to see her or hear a blow-by-blow account of their parting until the next day.

A whole afternoon to myself then. What should I do? Go through my desk and throw away all my high-school notes? Clean out my closet? Go for a long walk? Buy that new bikini I'd promised myself? Why did it have to be another whole week before Craig came home?

This is terrible, I thought, looking at myself in the mirror. *The third day of summer vacation and already you're bored!*

For want of something better to do, I began to put on new nail polish. I had only completed three fingers on the second hand when the doorbell rang. I went downstairs and tried to open the front door without touching the wet polish and smudged almost every finger.

"Yes?" I growled as I opened the front door.

"A fine way to greet a friend who's just been through a great emotional crisis," Toni said, sweeping into the hall and walking up the stairs ahead of me.

"Sorry," I said. "But I just smeared my nail polish. And I certainly wasn't expecting to see you. I thought you'd be off sobbing alone in some corner or throwing yourself off a bridge."

She turned and looked down at me, leaning easily against the banister and grinning as I walked up the stairs.

"I must say, you're looking very well for someone with a broken heart," I said.

"You know me," she said. "I always take things calmly. I never let my heart rule my head. So what if the greatest love of my life has gone half a world away? I'm strong. I'll survive."

"Toni," I said, climbing the last stair and putting my hands on both her shoulders. "I think my hearing must be defective. Have you been drinking, or have you sent a clone of yourself over?"

"I'm now mature enough to handle these situations," Toni said, looking very smug as she walked ahead of me into my room. "Is there any Coke, by the way—I'm so thirsty. Yelling above the noise of an airport isn't too good for your throat."

I went downstairs to get her a can. When I came back, she was seated at my vanity, putting on my red nail polish.

"So are you going to tell me all about it?" I asked.

"There's not much to tell," she said, picking up my final report card. "We said goodbye and he went. Hey, look at all these sickening A's. You really are a brain."

"Just like that, Toni?" I insisted. "He didn't say he'd miss you or anything?"

"No, he didn't say that," Toni said. "He didn't have to. Oh, great, you got an A in French. That's terrific."

"I suppose you want me to write your love letters for you," I said.

She looked up with that cheeky grin of hers. "No, I want you to do all the talking."

"When?" I asked suspiciously. Toni's eyes suddenly lit up with that wild, excited look she always gets at the beginning of one of her schemes.

"When we go to France this summer," Toni said, calmly putting the finishing touches on her nails.

"Would you mind repeating that?" I asked politely, "I don't think I heard you right."

"Watch my lips," Toni said. "I said that you and I were going to France this summer."

I shook my head slowly. "Toni, you can't chase a boy halfway around the world, you know."

She gave me this knowing smile. "For your information, I'm not chasing. He invited me to come and stay with him."

"Wow," I said. "I had no idea—I mean, I knew you two were, well, interested in each other, but I didn't know he was serious about you."

"You see," Toni said, grinning even wider, "you don't know everything about me, Jill Gardner." She put the nail polish down on the edge of my vanity. Too near the edge, and we both let out a little scream as it fell, open topped, and landed, miraculously, in my wastebasket. Another fact I haven't mentioned about Toni is that she's very accident prone.

"Sorry," she said sheepishly, rescuing the remaining nail polish from the wastebasket, which now looked as if it had been the site of a very nasty battle.

"It's OK," I said. "I don't think I'll ever be the type who wears red anyway. So go on. When did he invite you?"

"To tell you the truth," Toni said, "I was just as surprised as you are. I mean, I never thought of Philippe as the faithful kind. I went to the airport all prepared for a dramatic goodbye scene, and instead of that he suggested I come visit him this summer. So get your things packed and get out your French dictionary—"

"There's just one thing, Toni," I said, interrupting her firmly. "He invited you, not me. I have my summer all planned, and the plans do *not* include a trip to Europe that I can't afford."

Toni turned her wide blue eyes on me. "But I can't go on my own," she said.

"I don't see why not," I said. "It wouldn't exactly be a fun summer for me, sitting there while you and Romeo gaze and sigh at each other. Besides, as I said, I can't afford to go to Europe, and I've made plans for the summer."

"Well, I can't afford to go to Europe either,"

Toni said. "But it won't cost much more than our fare because we'll be staying with Philippe most of the time. And we can stop over in Paris on the way and see the Eiffel Tower and all the nightclubs. And think of the culture! Days in the museums and churchs, the opera, the Folies Bergère—"

I grabbed her arm. "I know you too well, Toni. You'd head straight for Philippe, and I'd spend my entire European vacation sitting in a corner. Besides, I don't want to go, even if I could afford it."

"You don't want to go to Europe?" Toni demanded. "Don't you realize that your education isn't complete until you've traveled abroad? Jill Gardner, this is terrible. I can just see you now—you'll go through college, marry Craig, and turn out just like your sister Stephanie, with a suburban house, a station wagon, two point one kids, and a dog."

"Don't forget the goldfish," I said, grinning at Toni's angry face. "Stephanie had goldfish, too. And, anyway, is her life so very terrible? It sounds OK to me, especially the marrying Craig part."

"But you're too young to think of settling down with one person," Toni said. "You need to experience life with a capital *L* before you decide to settle down."

I smiled at her as she paced up and down and wagged a finger at me. "You don't fool me one bit, Toni Redmond," I said evenly. "You don't care whether I turn into a boring person or not. All you care about is not having to travel to Europe by yourself."

Toni shrugged her shoulders. "So what if I'm scared to go through France on my own, with my C-minus French? What do you care? Some best friend you are. I can just see you a few years from now, telling your two point one kids, "Ah, yes, I remember Toni. She used to be my best friend. I wonder what happened to her? She was last seen heading for France alone—obviously came to a bad end.""

"Oh, Toni," I said, giving a long sigh. "You really are a pain sometimes. Look, I can understand that you don't want to travel by yourself. And I do want to see Europe someday before I end up as a boring housewife. But I really don't have the money this summer. And my folks don't have it, either. Besides, I already have a job lined up, and I don't want to leave Craig alone for a whole summer."

"OK," Toni said in a small voice. "I understand. Don't come then. I'll go alone, although I doubt if I'll even make it across Paris by myself." And before I could say another word, she had run down the stairs and out through the front door.

Of course, the moment she left I felt terrible that I'd let her down. I knew she was trying once again to manipulate me into doing something I didn't want to do, but I couldn't stop feeling guilty. And I knew this was how Toni always got her own way.

"This time you won't give in," I said. "She wants to chase some boy to Europe. Let her. You have your own life to lead. She must realize you're not her pet dog who comes whenever she calls."

But right after the pep talk, I went back to feeling guilty again.

Chapter Two

After she'd gone, I sat staring at myself in the mirror, feeling uneasy and upset. I wasn't uneasy because Toni had left in a huff: she'd done her famous walkout so many times that I was used to it. My uneasiness came from all the talk about going to Europe. Going to Europe with just one girlfriend was a very grown-up thing to do. It went with graduating from high school and being considered an adult. But I really didn't feel like an adult at all. In fact, the more I thought about it, the more I wanted to be safely back in high school. I could survive pretty well there, but I wasn't sure about the outside world, and even less sure about Paris, France.

So while I sat and stared at the mirror, part of me whispered, "Coward! Go with Toni and see the world!" Another part cursed her for letting out all these unsettled feelings just when I was beginning to feel in command of my future. I thought about Craig and how he'd be home in a few days and all the wonderful things we'd do together. The thought of Craig without me for a summer was more than I could bear. Even faithful, wonderful Craig wouldn't stay home alone. He was too good-looking; girls were waiting to snap him up.

"That settles it," I said out loud. "Nothing will make me leave Craig this summer. Toni will have to go alone." Then I remembered that she'd been my best friend for a lot longer than Craig had been my boyfriend, and I felt confused again. I had sudden visions of Toni lost on the Paris subway, kidnapped by evil Frenchmen, falling into the Seine . . .

"Darn her," I muttered. "Why does she always have to stir things up so that I don't know where I am or what I want?"

At dinner I told my parents all about Toni's latest wild scheme.

"Is she traveling all the way to France alone?" my mother asked.

"Actually," I said, playing with my roll and watching the crumbs fall onto the tablecloth, "she wants me to go with her."

"You mean you'd be staying with Philippe's family, too?" my mother asked. "Europe would be a wonderful experience for you. Did he expect her to bring a friend along?"

"She seems to think it would be fine," I said.

"Let's wait and see what his family has to say," Dad said. "I take it she'll be writing to them with all the details?"

They were both encouraging me to go! I couldn't believe it. I looked from one traitor's face to the other. "But what about the money?" I asked. "You know how much college is going to cost."

"But if you have an invitation to stay with Philippe," my mother said, "we could swing it. You provide your spending money, and we'll take care of the plane ticket."

"But you don't have to do that," I pleaded. "You said yourselves that you haven't got money to spare right now."

My father smiled, his wonderful super-Dad smile. "Your mother and I are very proud of your achievements in high school," he said. "And we haven't given you a graduation present yet. We'd planned to help you buy a car to take to college, as you know, but this trip is a once-in-a-lifetime opportunity!"

"I'd rather have the car," I muttered under my breath. Out loud I asked, "So you really won't worry if Toni and I wander around Europe on our own?" Were these the same parents who always came in person to drive me home after a party and made me file a flight plan every time I went to McDonalds?

They both gave me smiles of complete confidence. "It's not exactly going to be wandering around on your own, is it?" my mother said. "You'll be with a family. You're a mature young lady now. We're sure you can handle it."

No, I can't, I felt like yelling. *I don't think I can cope with not being a kid anymore. I'm scared to go to Europe by myself. I want to be back in kindergarten and hold your hand all the way.* But I didn't say that. Instead, I said, "But I'm really not sure that I want to go. I mean, I had my summer all planned out."

My mother went on smiling. "Oh, I'm sure they can find a replacement for you at day camp, Jill. She wouldn't want you to miss such a wonderful opportunity."

"Indeed not," my dad said heartily, giving a real-life impersonation of a father on an old TV sitcom. "Opportunities like this may only come once in a lifetime."

"There's another thing," I said hesitantly. "I don't know whether I want to leave Craig alone all summer."

From the glance that passed between them, I could tell that this was exactly why they wanted to get rid of me. I heard my mother talking about it the next day on the phone to Stephanie when she thought I was out watering the garden.

"So, of course, we were delighted," she was

saying as I came in through the kitchen door. "I mean, Craig is a very nice boy. We have nothing against him, but I can't help worrying that things are getting much too serious between them. She has four years of college ahead of her and then a career to think of. We don't want her thinking of getting married too young, do we? . . . Yes, Stephanie, I know you married at twenty . . . Yes, Stephanie, I know you're very happy, but then you were never very keen on studying, were you? For you it was the best thing. For Jill it would be a disaster. Maybe if she has a chance to see the world a little, she'll realize how much there's to do before she settles down. And maybe she and Craig will drift apart, which wouldn't be a bad thing either!"

I slipped past the kitchen door without being seen and crept up the stairs to my room. "Too bad, Toni," I muttered angrily. "I'm not going anywhere this summer, and I don't intend to drift apart from Craig—ever!"

Craig arrived home on Saturday morning. I was just helping load the dishwasher when I heard the pop-popping of his VW. I flew out the front door to meet him.

"Wow, what a reception," he said, laughing as I flung myself into his arms. "Anyone would think I had been away for years. I was only up for your prom three weeks ago!"

"I know," I said. "But I've missed you. I don't

16

suppose you miss me much with all those sophisticated college girls around you all the time and those coed dorms."

He held me tightly to him and, suddenly serious, gazed down at me. "I've missed you, too," he said in his low, deep voice. Then he kissed me, right out there in the street outside my house.

"We'd better not do too much of this when my parents are around," I said as we drew apart. "They're worried that we've been going together too long."

"So what're they going to do, lock you in your room or find you some other interest in life— underwater basket weaving, maybe?"

I had to smile. "Worse than that," I said. "They want me to go to Paris."

"Paris, France?" he asked, surprised.

I nodded. "Toni's been invited for the summer by that French exchange student—you know, the one in the play—and she doesn't want to travel alone."

"Terrific," Craig said. "I wish I could spend the summer in France, you lucky person."

I suddenly had this vision of Craig and me, walking hand in hand together along the Seine. "Why don't you come, too?" I asked. "Toni's going to be spending all her time with Philippe anyway. You and I could explore France together—that'd be wonderful."

He smiled down at me. "Yes, it would be nice. But I'm afraid I can't come, Jill. You know I've already agreed to go back to the modeling agency this summer, and I really need the money—"

"Then I'm not going either," I said. "I don't want to leave you for the whole summer, especially when you have to work."

Craig looked the slightest bit embarrassed. "I'd go to France if I were you," he said, "because, you see—I'm not going to be here for the summer."

"What do you mean, Craig?" I asked, stunned. "But you said you were going to work for that same modeling agency again."

"I know," he said. "And I *am* going to work for them. Remember I told you they asked me a few weeks ago if I was interested in a special two-month assignment?"

"And we were making jokes about it being a store mannequin!" I said.

"Well, I called them yesterday," Craig said. "And now they have the details. It's up in Alaska."

"Alaska?" I shouted. "What on earth can you model in Alaska—besides sealskins for Eskimos?"

He laughed, still a little uneasy. "They're going to be shooting a movie up there, and I've been hired as an extra."

"Wow, a movie," I said. "I've been dating a movie star! I hope you still remember me when you're rich and famous and far away in Alaska.'

I'd intended to make that a light remark. I hadn't intended my voice to wobble the way it did.

Craig looked down at me and stroked my hair. "Hey, don't look like that," he said. "You don't have anything to worry about. It's one of these survival-in-the-wilderness movies. I'll be alone up there with about fifty men and a few wolves and musk oxen. Nothing exciting—just a lot of hard work."

"The director is bound to have a pretty secretary," I said. "They always do."

He smiled then. "And the secretary wouldn't look twice at me when there are stars like Clint Eastwood around. Besides—I wouldn't look twice at the secretary. So don't worry."

"Who's worrying?" I asked, determined to keep the mood light. "I'll be surrounded by handsome Frenchmen—drifting down the Seine in the moonlight—"

"So you've decided to go now, have you?" he asked teasingly.

"Why not?" I said. "There's nothing to stay here for now, and I've always wanted to see the Mona Lisa."

Chapter Three

Once I'd made the decision, life suddenly speeded up alarmingly. There were plane tickets to book, clothes to pack, Paris guidebooks to read. Toni had found a student guidebook to Paris, and my parents studied it with me from cover to cover, deciding which hotels might be suitable for two young girls to stay in overnight. Apparently Philippe would not be meeting us at the airport after all. Everything happened in such a rush that it was almost as if I were watching a movie of some other girl planning for Europe.

Toni's brother eased our financial worries by finding out about a student charter flight that had a couple of cancellations.

*   *   *

Craig had to leave two days before I did. He was flying out in a chartered plane at six in the morning, and however much I loved him, I was not driving out to some airstrip at five in the morning. So I went over to his house to say goodbye the evening before.

"Have a great time, won't you?" he said, wrapping me in his arms. "And think of me surrounded by wolves."

"From what I hear of Paris," I said, "I'll be surrounded by even more wolves than you."

"Don't talk to them," he said. "Museums and churches only. Understand?"

"Only if you agree not to talk to the producer's secretary and the makeup girl," I said.

"They'll think I'm weird if I don't talk to them," he said. "But I promise to keep the conversation businesslike."

"I'll write every day," I said.

He laughed. "I bet you won't. You'll write for the first three days. Then you'll be having such a good time that you'll forget all about me."

"I will not!" I said angrily.

He touched my hair, stroking it back gently. "Look, Jill," he said. "I want you to have a great time this summer. I want you to see and experience as much as possible. And if you're too busy to write, I'll understand. We have to give each other space. I'll write to you as often as I can, but I can't promise to write every day. I might be

21

incredibly busy. You know what movies are like."

"I can guess," I said miserably.

"Hard work and long hours, I mean," he said sternly. "Not enjoying myself like you!"

"I don't know if I'll enjoy myself if you're not there," I said.

"Of course you will," he said. "I'm not the only thing in your life, you know. You can have a good summer without me. It may even be the best summer in your life."

I wasn't at all sure of that. As I drove home I felt uneasy about Craig. He didn't seem to think it was any big thing to be apart for a couple of months. He was obviously looking forward to Alaska, and he expected me to be looking forward to France. He said we both needed space. Was he feeling trapped in a relationship with me? I just hoped that by the end of this summer he'd realize that he missed me as much as I was going to miss him!

I stopped over at Toni's on the way home, feeling that I needed a dose of her bubbling enthusiasm.

"Oh, great, I'm so glad you're here," she said, greeting me at the door.

"I've just come from a fond farewell with Craig," I said as I stepped inside. "I need a little cheering up."

"You can be cheered up while you sit on my

22

suitcase," Toni said. "I can't get it closed, and everyone else is out."

"I sometimes get the feeling that you only keep me as a friend so that I'm around to sit on suitcases, do French homework, and escort you across the world," I said, following her upstairs.

She looked back and grinned. "Why else do people have friends?" she asked. "Here, look at this. It's impossible."

She opened the door to reveal a normal-sized suitcase, piled about two feet above its sides.

"No wonder you can't get it shut," I said, shaking my head in disbelief. "It's way too full. You can't take all this stuff with you."

"But I need it all," Toni wailed. "It's essential to my survival."

By the time I had finished taking out Toni's nonessentials and repacking, the case shut beautifully and I was no longer feeling depressed. In fact, that closed suitcase suddenly brought home to me that in two days I was actually going to fly across the world to a new country.

"I tell you what," I said. "Tomorrow you can come and help me pack and get your revenge!"

Then we were actually driving to the airport. I watched all the familiar landmarks flash past while I sat on the edge of my seat and tried to breathe normally.

"Now, we don't expect you to write every day, Jill," my mother said. "But for heaven's sakes let us know you've arrived safely and give us an address to write to."

"And you can always telephone if you need to," my father added.

"And remember," my mom added, "only take a taxi with a meter in Paris. I hear they're the most awful crooks over there."

My parents kept up a constant stream of good advice and cheerful chatter, not seeming to notice that I could only answer in grunts.

For once in her life Toni arrived before me. She looked cute and excited and not at all nervous. "You'll never guess who phoned before I left," she said, dragging me aside while our parents went over details together. "Good old Rich! He told me to take care and that he still loves me. He even asked for my address so that he could write. Wasn't that sweet of him?"

"You have nerve, Toni Redmond," I said. "Getting one boy to write to you at another boy's house!"

"Oh, I didn't give him Philippe's address," Toni said. "I told him that my mother would forward letters since I didn't always know where we'd be."

"What did you mean by that?" I asked sharply. "Aren't we going to be at Philippe's the whole time?"

"I guess so," she said, looking past me at the departure board. "But in case we aren't . . ."

"What do you mean, in case we aren't?" I demanded. "You told me you'd heard from him. He does know we're coming, doesn't he?"

"Sort of," she said. "Hey, look, our flight is ready for boarding. Let's go!" Then she dashed off ahead of me, hugging parents and brothers, tripping over people's luggage, leaving me to follow behind, wondering if I was crazy to let her drag me halfway across the world to an uncertain destination!

"Do you remember that song about Paris when it drizzles?" Toni asked, forcing a giggle.

"Most amusing," I said dryly.

"Well, at least it feels like home," she said.

"If I'd wanted rain I could've saved the air fare and stayed in Seattle," I said, pulling my cotton jacket up around my neck in a useless attempt to keep out the most stinging raindrops. "How come your guidebook didn't warn people to bring their ski clothes along?"

"I wanted to bring my ski clothes, remember. You were the one who stopped me. Now wait and see. When everything is flooded tomorrow, you'll wish I'd brought flippers, too!"

I frowned at her.

"Oh, don't be such an old grouch," Toni said. "We're here, aren't we? We're actually in the middle of Paris, and we got here safely, and the wings didn't fall off, and the engines didn't cut out, and nobody hijacked us, and we even landed at the right airport."

"I know," I said, managing a weak smile. "But I can't help feeling like a grouch. My stomach still feels as if it's at thirty thousand feet, and my eyes feel as though they're about to pop out of my head."

"You should've made yourself eat," Toni said. "Then you wouldn't have felt so sick. The steak was delicious. So was that whipped cream pudding."

I shuddered at the thought of it. Frothy and quivering, it had sat there until Toni snatched it from my tray and ate it, the way she had eaten the rest of my meal. All I had managed were some crackers and tea. Now I felt as if I hadn't eaten for a week.

"So what do we do now?" I asked, shivering as a gust of wind buffeted us. We were standing on a corner in the middle of Paris, where the airline bus had deposited us. We hadn't a clue as to where we were. We'd tried looking at our map, but the wind pulled at it, all but snatching it from our hands. It was evening rush hour, and millions of tiny cars streamed past us, all with their lights on—though it wasn't yet dark—and all madly honking their horns. People rushed up and down the sidewalks, elegantly dressed people with umbrellas, talking loudly and all looking as if they belonged here and knew where they were going. On the opposite side of the street was an old building that looked like a palace, but a sign indicated that it was a railway station. Grubby trees lined the street, each with a metal cage around it. A magazine kiosk was covered in plastic to keep the rain out, and the man inside it was wearing a real French beret. It was the sort of scene we'd looked at in travel books. Now it was real and rain-streaked and old. I didn't dare admit to Toni that I wanted to turn around and go straight home again.

Toni struggled to get out her little book. "We'd better take a taxi to the hotel," she said.

"Tell me again. Where does it say the hotel is?" I asked, shivering.

"Over in the student quarter," Toni said vaguely. "That can't be too far from here."

"I wish you could have phoned Philippe from the airport the way I said. Then he could've come and met us." I shifted my luggage out of the way of a spout of water that cascaded from the roof.

Toni growled, the way she did if you tried to push her too far. "I told you he lives a hundred miles away," she said. "And that's not like a hundred miles in America. It takes him all day to drive to Paris. Besides"—she let her voice trail off as she stared out into the distance—"I didn't exactly let him know we were coming."

"He doesn't even know we're coming?" I

shrieked, clutching at her arm. "Are you trying to tell me we've come halfway around the world and the guy doesn't even know we're coming? But you told me you'd written to him, Toni Redmond! Do you mean to say you lied to me?"

"Only because I knew you probably wouldn't come if it wasn't all arranged before we left home," she said.

"But why didn't you write, Toni?" I had that horrible sinking feeling in my stomach that always appears during any of Toni's crazier moments.

Toni shook the rain off her curls. "There was really no need, that's why," she said casually. "I kept telling you—it's an open invitation for the summer."

"But what if he's not even there, Toni?"

"You don't invite somebody if you're not going to be there," she said. "Anyway, he told me he has to work on his father's farm all summer."

"Great," I said. "So we get to spend an entire summer mucking out the pigs!"

"You're being an old grouch again," Toni said. "Just think—you're in Paris, France, and even you have to admit this is better than playing ring-around-a-rosy with twenty little five-year-olds."

I shook my head. "Toni, why did I ever get mixed up with you?"

"Because life was too boring without me?" she

asked, giving me her sweetest smile. "Come on, let's just get safely to the hotel. It's bound to be full of nice, friendly students who can tell us where to eat. Everything will be fine."

Chapter Four

We stood at the curb, waving like crazy people, and pretty soon a taxi actually stopped for us.

"Hôtel des Étoiles, Rue Picard," Toni read from the book. She had to repeat it twice before he seemed to understand.

"You go to hotel? Rue Picard?" he asked, looking worried. "I think you make the mistake, no?"

"No," Toni said. "See, it says here in the book. Rue Picard."

He shrugged his shoulders. "I know not the hotel," he said. "But if you wish, I take you."

A few minutes later we were squashed into the backseat with our luggage, clinging to each other as we screeched around corners of Paris.

"They all drive like maniacs over here," Toni whispered.

"And I was worried about the wing falling off the airplane," I whispered back as we crossed eight lanes of traffic, causing every car on the street to start blowing its horn again. "That was nothing compared to this!" Soon we left the wide avenues and bright lights behind. We drove through dark, narrow streets and around lots of tight corners. Even if we had had a sense of direction to start with, we would have lost it. Finally we turned into a street, darker and narrower than any of the others.

"Rue Picard," the driver said, looking back at us.

We both peered out into the gloom. "Are you sure?" I asked. "There isn't more than one Rue Picard?"

"Only one," he said. "What number you desire?"

Toni peered at the book again. "Twenty-five," she said.

"*Voilà*, twenty-five," the driver said. We paid, too tired and dim-witted to know if he had overcharged us. Then we climbed out. The driver roared away, and there we were, standing alone in a smelly alley. One lone street lamp splashed a pool of light on the cobblestones, and by this we could read a small, peeling sign above the door, Hôtel des Étoiles.

"This can't be it," Toni said, in a very quiet voice for her.

"It's the right address," I said. "Maybe it's just the outside that looks bad. Maybe it's friendly upstairs. Anyway, we can't stand here in the street getting soaked." I walked ahead of her up the front steps and rang the bell.

The door was opened an inch or so, and a fat face with a drooping mustache peered around it, took one look at us, and scowled.

"We want a room for the night," I said in what I hoped was my best French.

The face kept scowling. "You Americans?" he asked in English.

We nodded.

"Hmmph," he said.

"Do you have a room?" I asked. I was standing directly beneath an impressive water spout that was running down the back of my neck.

"I don't want no trouble," he said. "No men in the rooms. No drugs. Understand?"

"Of course we understand," I said, suddenly feeling very angry. "Now can we come in? We're getting very wet. Your hotel was in an American student guide, you know."

"I know," he said, opening the door. "And since then all I get is trouble. I don't want no trouble. Understand?"

"Cheerful guy," Toni muttered as we signed in at the front desk. "Makes you feel real welcome."

"Bound to have a heart of gold underneath," I

whispered back, and we both giggled. This made the man scowl even more.

"Room twenty-four," he said. "Top floor."

"Can we have some help with our baggage?" Toni asked, dragging her large case across the floor.

"We have the elevator, mademoiselle," the man said, giving Toni a withering look and pointing to an iron cage behind us.

We took the key and dragged our cases into it. After we pressed the button, it started to rise very slowly, making terrible creaking and groaning noises. Toni gave me a sideways look.

"I've seen elevators like this in movies," she said. "They always get stuck between floors, and when they finally come up, there's a corpse in them."

"Thanks a lot," I said. "You sure know how to reassure a person."

Luckily this one did not get stuck. But it took hours to reach the top floor while we stood, dripping on the floor and shivering, half from fright and half from cold.

As we opened the door to our room and turned on the light, something scurried across the floor.

"I don't like this place, Toni," I said, hesitating to walk in farther. "Why didn't we just go to the Hilton?"

"Maybe it was the hundred-dollar-a-night difference in price," Toni suggested, walking boldly in and flinging her bag onto one bed. "And, anyway, it's only for a couple of nights. Soon we'll be staying at Philippe's comfortable farmhouse, eating good home cooking."

"Shut up," I said. "I'm starving. Let's have a shower, then go out to eat, shall we?"

"Just one minor problem," Toni said. "We don't seem to have a shower."

"Oh," I said. "Maybe we have to share one."

We crept down the hall together, listening to all the floorboards madly creaking, and finally located a bathroom at the end.

"That's what I call togetherness," Toni said. "One bathroom for the whole floor."

"Well, at least nobody else seems to be around right now," I said. "Why don't we have a quick shower while we can."

"OK," Toni said. "You can go first. I need to unpack to find my shampoo."

I grabbed my toilet bag and left her humming to herself as she threw items all over her bed. Toni is not a tidiness freak!

The first thing I noticed, after I locked the door of the bathroom was that there was no shower, only a huge old tub on claw feet and above it a horrible tank sort of thing with pipes coming out in all directions. The tub was an interesting green color in the bottom, but right then I was too wet and cold to care. I put in the stopper and turned on the hot water. A great *whoosh* of flame shot out above my head, and the tank thing began to rattle and shake and clank and hiss until it finally sent forth a trickle of scalding water that settled in the bottom of the tub.

"I don't think I'll bother," Toni said when I told her all the horrible details of bathing in three inches of water. "I'd rather eat, I think. Our first meal of French food! What shall we have—escargots? Pâté de foie gras? I hope your French is good enough to order for us. I'm starving."

My French was not feeling good at all. In fact, as we rode down in the elevator, all I could remember were words like bread and water. If my vocabulary didn't come back rapidly, we were in for a dull meal. We walked down the alley and out into a brightly lit street.

"What about this?" Toni asked, peering into the window of a candle-lit restaurant.

"I don't know," I said. "Looks expensive. Besides, I wouldn't know what to order."

We saw a couple of others, but they looked rather frightening and expensive, too.

"I really want a proper French meal," Toni said. "It's got to be good for our first night here."

Then we turned a corner, and there ahead of us was a magnificent sight—golden arches twinkled above the wet pavement.

"Toni, look!" I said. "Do you see what I see?"

She nodded, eyes shining.

"Of course, I know you wanted a real French meal, so if you'd rather go somewhere else . . ." I said.

"Are you kidding?" she yelled. "Right now I would do anything in the world for a Big Mac and fries. What are we waiting for?"

We both crossed the street at a run.

Chapter Five

The amazing thing was that, in spite of the lumpy bed, the mouse or whatever we had seen scurrying across the floor, and the loud noises coming up from the street behind us, I slept like a log. When I woke the next morning, the sun was painting a bright square of light on the wall behind me. Toni was already up and standing at the window.

"Hey, come and look at this," she called.

I walked over to her. "Wow," I said. Our hotel was on a hill, and the whole city of Paris lay below us, twinkling in the morning sunshine. We could even see the glint of the river between buildings. The Eiffel Tower looked enormous and almost close enough to touch.

"Now aren't you glad we came?" Toni asked as

if she were the magician who had produced this scene for my benefit.

"It's just like in all the pictures," I said, feasting on it. "Look, there's Notre Dame Cathedral, and that wide street must be the Champs Élysées. And isn't that the Arc de Triomphe?"

"What are we waiting for?" Toni asked. "Let's get out and explore."

We dressed quickly, grabbed our student guide to Paris, our cameras and purses, then waited, bursting with impatience, as the elevator sank at a snail's pace to the ground floor.

"Good morning!" Toni sang out to the proprietor, who was slurping coffee at his desk.

"Hmmph," he said, scowling up at us.

"Nice guy," Toni said as we went out into the sunshine. "I hope not all Frenchmen are as friendly as he is."

"From what I've always heard, most of them are too friendly," I said.

"Philippe is very friendly," Toni said. "I can't wait to see him again. I hope he's been missing me desperately and he grabs me passionately as I step off the train."

"And I hope you remember that you've got me around," I said dryly. "I'm easily embarrassed, you know."

Toni flashed me her cheeky grin. "Then we'll just have to find someone for you," she said. "Maybe Philippe has a cousin or something."

"I don't think Craig would like that," I said.

"Well, I don't think he's got anything to complain about," she said. "You don't know what he's doing in Alaska. I understand the girls up there are real friendly, too! Besides, you need a wild, passionate romance once in a while. You and Craig are getting to be like a boring old married couple."

"You concentrate on you and Philippe," I told her as we walked down a flight of steep steps. "And don't try finding a guy for me. For me this is purely a cultural vacation, plus a mercy mission to make sure you get back home in one piece." As I said the last part of the sentence, I grabbed at Toni before she could step out in front of a speeding taxi.

"You make it sound like I'm some sort of idiot who needs looking after," Toni said indignantly, then promptly stepped off the curb and into a puddle.

"I rest my case," I said, laughing.

We found the nearest Metro, or subway, station and managed to buy a token and get on the train in the right direction for downtown. Then, feeling like experienced world travelers, we managed to get off again at the Champs Élysées. We came up to the surface, and the experienced world travelers disappeared. In their place were two girls, freshly arrived from the States and awestruck by what we saw. Until that moment we *knew* all about the famous buildings in Paris, but now we *felt* them all around us. I guess growing up on the West Coast of the United States I tended to think that anything a hundred years old was pretty historic. Now I realized that we were in a city that had stood unchanged for hundreds and hundreds of years.

Toni must have been having the same thoughts. She was very quiet for a time, then she said in a whisper, "Do you realize that Napoleon walked down this very same street?"

"Perhaps even the Romans did," I suggested.

"I bet you're right," she said seriously. "You know, I think I saw a Roman cigarette package in the gutter back there?" Then she looked up and grinned. It was hard to squash Toni for long.

"So where do you want to go first?" I asked, looking in one direction up to the Arc de Triomphe and in the other down to the Place de la Concorde.

"How about shopping in the Galleries Lafayette?" Toni said, her eyes shining.

I sighed. "Your problem is that you have no sense of culture," I said. "We come to one of the most historic cities of the world, and all you want to do is go shopping."

"It's a very famous store," Toni said. "So what do you want to do?"

"I'd really like to see the Louvre," I said.

Toni sighed. "It's full of old things," she said. "See one old thing and you've seen them all."

"Toni, how can you say that?" I exclaimed.

She laughed. "I knew that would make you lose your cool," she said. "I tell you what. On the way back home when we stop in Paris again, you go to the Louvre while I go shopping."

"OK," I said. "Anyway, the weather is much too nice to spend the day in a museum. Why don't we go up the Eiffel Tower?"

"Great idea," Toni said. "Get out the map and we'll walk."

It was a beautiful walk, through some gardens and over the Seine, then more gardens. I kept on stopping to take pictures, and Toni kept on stopping to look around anxiously.

"What's the matter?" I asked at last.

"What if Philippe doesn't think I look good beside all these French girls?" she asked nervously.

"Will you stop worrying about how you look and enjoy the view?" I said. "Look at the Eiffel Tower. I had no idea it was so huge."

We stood together, small as ants under one of the giant legs. It made me dizzy to look up and up to where white clouds sailed above the top levels.

"I'm not sure I want to go up now," Toni said. "I just remembered that I'm afraid of heights."

"Oh, I'm sure it's very safe," I said. "It's all caged in up there, and you don't have to look down. And the view will be fantastic. Besides, imagine telling people you went to Paris and didn't go up the Eiffel Tower?"

"Well, I suppose I might faint into the arms of a cute boy up there," Toni said. "OK, let's get it over with."

"You make it sound like having a tooth pulled," I said, following her into the elevator.

We soared up and up, watching Paris slip away beneath us, then came out to a narrow platform.

"There's another elevator above this," I said. "That one goes right to the top."

Toni shuddered. "I really don't think I could face going any higher," she said. "And you have all the view you need from here."

She really did look pale and sick. I had had no idea that Toni was scared of anything, but then we'd never been up high together, except on a plane, and that didn't seem to count.

"Do you want to sit down?" I asked, pointing to the bench. "Then I'll just take a quick look around, and we can go down again."

She shook her head. "No, I'll come around with you, now that I'm here," she said. "I really shouldn't miss the view."

We walked around slowly, identifying things in our guide book, using up a whole roll of film, watching the city disappear into a haze in all directions. Neither of us had seen a city that large before. It was kind of alarming to see houses following more houses into infinity.

"I really didn't realize how high up I was until I looked directly down," I said, peering over the edge to watch the toy cars scurry along the road beneath us.

"You're right," Toni said, then suddenly she screamed. "Everything's swaying around," she said and wildly clutched at my arm. The only problem was that my arm was resting on the edge of the railing. As she clutched at me, she knocked the purse from my hand, and we both watched in horror as it plunged hundreds of feet to disappear from sight.

"My purse," I screamed hysterically, rushing for the elevator. "It's got everything in it—my passport, my tickets, my money—"

"I'm sorry," Toni screamed, running behind me. "I'm sorry, Jill. I didn't mean to— I just felt like I was going to faint, honestly I did."

I guess the other people in the elevator must have thought we were very weird, but to tell the truth, I didn't even notice them. I only had one thought in my mind—to reach that purse before someone picked it up and ran off with everything I owned.

The elevator stopped. I pushed a fat German lady out of the way, mowed down some waiting Japanese tourists, and sprinted in the direction of my purse, only vaguely hearing the shouts that followed me. Then a miracle happened—a dark, serious-looking young man was walking slowly toward me with my purse in his hands.

"My purse!" I shrieked again.

His eyes met mine. "This is yours, mademoiselle?" he asked in French.

"Oh, *oui*," I said, running toward him. "I thought I'd lost it forever. I'm sorry. I don't speak French too well."

His whole face broke into a smile. "Neither do I," he said. "I'm Italian. I am a student here, but my French is still bad. My English is much better. I worked in London last year."

"Terrific," I said, beaming at him as he handed the purse to me. "You don't know how relieved I am that someone found this."

"I could not help but find it," he said. "Since it almost struck me on the head."

I realized for the first time what damage a flying purse dropped from a few hundred feet could do. "Oh, I'm so sorry," I said. "I hope it didn't hurt you."

He smiled again. He had a wonderful smile. His eyes really sparkled, and his whole face seemed to glow. "Luckily," he said, "it did not strike me. It fell right before me. I was walking along and suddenly—boom—there it lands at my feet. I think to myself, What is this? Is this a gift from heaven?" His face suddenly became serious as his eyes met mine. "I think perhaps I was right," he said. "I think maybe it was heaven that arranged this. My name is Carlo. What is yours?"

"It's Jill," I said in a shaky voice.

"Jeel." He tried it once, rolling it around on his

tongue. "Jeel. A pretty name. You are American, no?"

"Yes," I said.

"And in Paris for long?"

"No. We leave tomorrow," I said.

"A great pity," he said. "I have to spend two more weeks here studying. I should have liked to show you Paris. It is a very romantic city."

I was almost ready to tell him that I'd changed my mind and was going to stay on when Toni went down to Philippe's. I shook myself back to reality. *What are you doing, Jill Gardner?* I demanded firmly of myself. *You're not the sort of girl who lets a strange guy pick you up—even if you did almost kill him with your purse. And even if he is very, very cute.*

To hide my embarrassment, I opened the purse and let out a gasp of horror. I had forgotten that my purse also contained my makeup. It had all smashed, and everything was covered in blue powder eye shadow, red lipstick, blusher, and tiny slivers of mirror. "Oh, no," I said. "Look, it's all over my passport and my tickets." I drew out my passport and started to wipe off the mess with a tissue.

"Here," Carlo said. "Use this. It is much bigger." He handed me a handkerchief.

"Oh, thanks," I said, scrubbing away madly at my passport cover. "I don't think the stain will ever come off. I wonder if they'll let me back into the States with a tie-dyed passport cover!"

"As long as the pretty face inside is untouched, all will be well," he said. "See, no real harm is done."

"And the rest of your stuff is in this plastic pouch," Toni said, wiping it off. "But I think the purse is a goner. You'll never get the slivers of glass out of it now. Just think, seven years bad luck, and it's all my fault."

"What is this seven years bad luck?" Carlo asked, looking alarmed.

"Just an old saying," I said. "You break a mirror, you get seven years of bad luck."

"Not true," he said fiercely. "In my country you get seven years of *good* luck, and it starts from today. Shall we go and have a coffee together to calm our nerves after the adventure of the flying purse?"

"Good idea," I said. "My knees are still trembling." Which was true, although I didn't think it was from the flying purse anymore. I went to hand him back his handkerchief, then saw that it was beige silk, now badly stained with lipstick.

"Oh, no," I said. "Your beautiful handkerchief. I had no idea—you shouldn't have lent it to me."

His face broke into that wonderful smile again. "And for what else do I carry around a useless silk handkerchief all these years—only to have it ready if a beautiful girl needs it one day. Come. I know a delightful coffee bar not far away."

Chapter Six

"You see," Toni said triumphantly as we left the café. "It was only a question of finding the correct way to make boys notice us in France. And obviously the correct way is to drop something on their heads. Next we can go and stand at the top of Notre Dame and throw your camera down, then lean over one of the bridges of the Seine and drop your jacket on a passing boat. It's much easier than fishing, and who knows what we'll catch?"

"Shut up, Toni," I said.

She threw me a quick look. "What's eating you? I thought you enjoyed meeting Carlo and having coffee with him. You looked like you enjoyed it. You were eager enough to meet him again tonight."

"That's the trouble," I said. "I did enjoy it. And it's not at all like me. I keep thinking I should have my head examined. Toni—we've agreed to go out tonight with a complete stranger. That's something we'd never do at home. We don't know anything about him."

"Except he's really cute looking," Toni said, throwing me a sideways glance.

"OK, so he's really cute."

"And he has beautiful manners and silk handkerchiefs, and he treated us to wonderful coffee and croissants, and he made himself a half hour late for class, even though we did nearly kill him."

"So you really think we can trust him?" I asked hesitantly.

She nodded. "Somebody like me, a woman of the world, experienced with men, has a feeling for the ones she can trust. And my feeling in this case is that we dropped your purse on the right guy. Besides, there's safety in numbers, and we're two, strong, red-blooded American girls— *and* we leave in the morning. So what have we got to lose?"

"You're right," I said. "I should learn to worry less. We'll have a great time tonight, and we'll leave in the morning. As you say, what have we got to lose?"

In spite of this I worried about it all day. We went up the tower of Notre Dame Cathedral from which the Hunchback had flung himself to his death. This time Toni wouldn't go near the edge, and we didn't drop my camera. We saw Napoleon's tomb and a lot of royal palaces and old churches and wonderful gardens. And all the time my mind only half took in the stained-glass windows and the rose beds and the elegant marble. The other half kept seeing a face with big, dark eyes that sparkled when he laughed and hearing a voice saying, "Jeel." I knew it was crazy to think about someone I'd never see again after that night. I knew that I really loved Craig, and I forced myself to picture him instead, but his face was a pale blur in my memory.

"Are you feeling OK?" Toni asked as we walked through the millionth park en route to the millionth palace.

"Sure," I said. "Why?"

"I don't know," she said, looking hard at me. "You haven't listened to half the things I've been saying. I was wondering if jet lag has caught up with you."

"My legs are feeling tired," I said. "And I'm hot. Otherwise, I'm fine. And I haven't listened to half the things you've said since second grade."

"You're not still thinking about what's-his-name?" she asked, pretending to look interested in the water splashing out of a fountain.

"Who, Carlo?" I asked, examining the same fountain carefully. "Well, I *was* still wondering if we're doing the right thing meeting him tonight."

"So you don't want to?" she asked, moving away as the wind changed and a fine curtain of spray fell on us.

"I didn't say that," I said. "I guess nothing much can happen walking around Paris."

"According to all the old movies, a lot can happen walking around Paris," Toni said. "People only have to stroll along the Seine for five minutes and they fall desperately in love."

"In the old movies," I said, brushing the spray from my hair. "Oh, that spray felt good. Does that look like an ice-cream stand over there? I'm really dying for something cool."

By about four o'clock our legs had finally given out, jet lag had caught up, and we couldn't walk another step.

"If I see another church, I'll scream," Toni said. "Let's go back to the hotel, and then you can help me prepare what to say when I phone Philippe. I think my French is coming along pretty well. I even ordered my own ice cream."

I didn't like to say that she had asked for strawberry and got chocolate, because she was trying hard.

"So long as you don't want me to phone Philippe," I said. "I don't mind helping you write your speech. Besides, you can explain the difficult part—like you're arriving *with* a friend, in a few hours—in English."

"I hope he's pleased to see me," Toni said, for once in her life not sounding sure of herself. She twisted a curl around her finger tighter and tighter, something she only did when very nervous.

"Of course he'll be pleased to see you," I said. "He'll be thrilled that you came all this way to be with him again. After all, he did invite you. He'd only do that if you were really special to him."

"Yes," she said, still twisting her hair. "All the same, I wish tomorrow was already over."

Miraculously we found our way back to the hotel. Nothing scurried when we opened the door. The view across the city was still spectacular. Toni went to the bathroom first, and I sat in the window writing postcards. I quickly scribbled one off to my folks and to Stephanie's kids. But when it came to Craig's, I couldn't seem to find the right words. I was missing him, wasn't I? I did really wish he was here with me. In the end I just wrote, "Paris is even more beautiful than the pictures. Sorry we have to leave tomorrow. Hope you are having fun. Love, Jill." *Now why did I write that?* I wondered, staring at it. Did I really hope he was having fun? Surely I secretly hoped he was miserable and missing me, didn't I? I lay back on my bed and thought about Alaska—half a world away.

"That is without a doubt the world's worst bathroom," Toni said, waking me from a half sleep as she came back in. "Those pipes were groaning and clanking so much, I was terrified

51

they would drop on my head. And all that steam! I felt as if I was going to faint." She flung herself down on her bed and closed her eyes. "Actually," she said, "I'm not feeling at all well. Would you mind going on your own this evening?"

"What's wrong?" I asked in alarm. Toni was never sick. She was as strong as an ox.

"Nothing terrible," she said, pushing her hair back from her face. "I just don't feel good. I felt dizzy when I walked along the hall, and now my head's starting to ache. I think it's just tiredness. After all, we did a lot of walking today."

"But it's not like you to feel tired," I said. "You normally have to drag me behind you. I hope you're not coming down with the flu or something. Do you think we should get a doctor?"

"Will you stop panicking?" Toni said. "I guess I just have good, old-fashioned jet lag. I need a nice long sleep, and I'll feel terrific in the morning."

"What about Philippe? Don't you want to phone him tonight?"

"I don't think I feel up to it," she said in a weak voice. "I'll call in the morning, just before we get on the train."

"That's not exactly giving him much notice, Toni," I said.

"One night won't make much difference," Toni said. "And I really don't feel up to facing a phone call in French."

"I'll stay with you," I said.

52

"Don't be dumb," she said, opening her eyes. "Of course you have to go. We can't leave the poor guy waiting around and then not show up."

"But I don't know that I want to go if you aren't going," I said. "And I certainly don't want to leave you alone in this dump."

"For heaven's sake, go," Toni said. "All I want to do is sleep, so you can't do anything for me, and think of poor old Carlo waiting hopefully by the Arc de Triomphe. If we don't show up, he'll have a bad opinion of American girls. You don't want to let down our entire nation, do you?"

I laughed and got up. "You really are something," I said. "All right, I'll go. I don't suppose anything bad can happen to me right in the middle of Paris, and he really does seem to be a nice person."

I opened my suitcase and brought out one outfit after another. Everything seemed too casual for an evening in Paris. Finally I settled for my new gray jumpsuit, with the ankle-length pants.

"My," Toni said, after I was dressed. "We *are* aiming to impress, aren't we?"

"What do you mean?" I asked, turning my back to her and brushing my hair.

"The new outfit, never worn before," she said, propping herself up on one elbow. "The one we decided makes you look like a model. You must think the guy is special."

"It has nothing to do with Carlo," I said. "I just

53

feel you have to look elegant in Paris, and this is the most elegant thing I own."

"Well, you certainly look great," Toni said. "You almost make me wish I was coming along—all those boulevards and the lights on the Seine."

"Then come," I said. "I'll wait for you to get ready. You're looking much better."

"No, I still have a headache," Toni said. "I guess I'll wait to take romantic strolls with Philippe and his pigs."

"Do you want me to bring you some food before I go?" I asked, dropping my hairbrush into the tote bag I would have to use until I bought a new purse.

"No, thanks," Toni said. "If I feel like eating I know my way to McDonald's."

"Don't travel down in the elevator alone," I said.

"I don't plan to. If it got stuck between floors, I'd die of heart failure. Will you stop worrying about me?" Toni asked, sitting up and glaring at me. "Now get going, or Romeo will think you aren't coming."

Chapter Seven

He was standing at the top of the Metro steps, looking very dignified in a light suit. I was reminded of the first time I met Craig, when he also wore a business suit, and I thought him too young to be an executive. When Carlo saw me, his face broke into that smile again—a wonderful smile, as if this moment was the nicest thing that had happened to him in his entire life.

"Jeel," he said, stepping toward me. "I'm so glad you came. I worry when you are a little late." He looked around. "Where is the friend?"

"Toni wasn't feeling well," I said. "She decided to stay home. I hope you don't mind?"

His eyes met mine. "I am very sorry for Tonee that she does not feel well," he said, "but at the same time I am very happy that I have you all to myself this evening. It will be a special evening, I think. No?"

I didn't dare trust my voice, so I just smiled. We walked away from the Metro station together in silence, which wasn't hard because the street noises around us were so loud. I realized that I couldn't think of anything to say and felt a sudden panic—what if I couldn't think of a thing to say all evening? Back home I'd thought I'd become pretty mature and sophisticated. Now I felt like a little freshman again, out on my first date and scared I was going to make a fool of myself. I stole a glance at Carlo walking beside me. He was tall and slim and seemed very relaxed. He looked at everybody and everything that passed us as if the whole world was interesting to him.

We crossed to the Arc de Triomphe and stood quietly in the flickering torchlight at the Tomb of the Unknown Soldier.

"It upsets me to come here," Carlo said quietly. "I always think that this boy was no older than me. He probably did not even know what he was fighting for. And we don't even know his name." He turned and started to walk out from the arch.

"So many people have died in so many wars," he said. "And most of them have died for nothing. So stupid for countries to make war. They should leave everything to us young people. We know how to make friends very well, don't we, Jeel?"

He took my hand as he steered me through the traffic. Once we were on the sidewalk again, he released my hand. He talked easily, one minute about very serious things, like war and politics and communism, the next he was making a joke about a strangely dressed person we passed. I had never met anyone like him before.

"So what are the things that worry you and your friends at home?" he asked me suddenly.

"I don't know," I said, stumbling over the words, uncertain as to what kind of answer he expected. He had talked about some serious things. "Well—it's scary to think of being an adult suddenly."

"You're right," he said, nodding in agreement. "Who wants to grow up and worry about things? Much better to stay young and play, no? We will talk of no more serious things this evening!"

Then we laughed as we walked down the Champs Élysées and past the expensive stores. We laughed at the thousand-dollar dresses that were so ugly and the hundred-dollar bottles of perfume that were so small. We stopped to eat at a sidewalk café, and Carlo ordered me an omelette before I could tell him that I hated them. But the omelette that came was nothing like the flabby mounds of egg I was familiar with. It was light and fluffy and full of mushrooms and melted cheese. It slipped down easily enough, although I hadn't felt particularly hungry.

All the time we sat at the café, Carlo talked. He told me about his life as a student in Paris. He said he found it a very hard and unfriendly city compared to his own. The students had to work so hard to pass their exams that they shut themselves away and studied all the time.

"But I do not take the studying so seriously," Carlo said. "After all, what a waste of life to sit all day in a library! My father, he says he wants me to learn French, so I say I will go to Paris. Fine. Now I can speak a little French, and he will have to be satisfied with that."

"But what will you do now?" I asked. "Do you have to go back to college at home?"

He laughed again. "If I can ever decide what subject I should study," he said. "But my father, he does not want me to study. He wants me to join him in his business so that I can take it over someday."

"What kind of business?"

"He has a glass-blowing factory. You know that Venice is famous for glass. He makes beautiful things."

"But you don't want to join him?"

"Would you like to work with your father all day long?" he asked. "All day he will tell me what to do. Besides, I do not like glass. It is very hot and dirty in the factory. I like the fresh air and people—and no hard work. All I really want to be is a writer, and the only experience I need for that is life."

We left the café and crossed the street into the Tuileries gardens. It was funny to think that a few hours before I had been scared to spend the evening with him, without Toni there to protect me. I had decided on the subway coming into town that I would stick to well-lighted streets and crowds of people, just to be on the safe side. Yet here we were walking through the darkened gardens, and I wasn't worried at all.

It was a warm, scented night. City noises drifted across to us—a burst of music, frantic honking of horns, a screech of brakes—but they were muffled as if they came from very far away. Our feet scrunched over gravel, and every now and then we caught the perfume of unseen roses close by.

"Where is everybody?" I asked, conscious suddenly that we heard no other scrunching over gravel.

I saw his flash of white teeth as he smiled. "Most tourists are very sensible," he said. "They do not dare walk through the darkened gardens at night, in case something terrible happens to them." He turned and looked at me, patted my shoulder in a brotherly way, then smiled again. "But you do not have to worry, little Jeel. I am here to protect you from all bad Parisian men."

"But what about bad Italians?" I asked, feeling

reassured by that smile. "Can I trust those, do you think?"

"Of course," he said quickly. "Italians are always honorable."

"That's not what we hear in America," I said. "Italians are supposed to be always chasing after girls."

"That is what we hear about American boys," he said, his eyes twinkling. "And now you know that both are wrong. I think you will learn much in Europe."

We came out at last onto the banks of the Seine, where the water flowed black and gurgling and smelled of weeds. The air in the city had been still, but here a cool breeze swept my hair back. Small lamps dotted the embankment at intervals, and rows of lights showed where the bridges were. A brilliantly lit tourist boat drifted by with music blaring. After it had passed, everything seemed very still and quiet, as if we had stepped into a private world.

"This is my favorite part of Paris," Carlo said, leaning over the river wall and looking down into the black water. "It is very romantic, no?"

I felt a tiny shiver of alarm. He had acted like a perfect gentleman until now. Had he just been waiting for a deserted spot like this?

"Yes, I guess it's romantic," I said, staring out across the water. I suddenly remembered standing on the quay at home, feeling the salt spray on my lips as Craig kissed me.

"You think perhaps of your loved one who is now far away?" Carlo asked in a gentle voice. "And wish that he could be here beside you?"

"Yes," I said. "I was thinking about him. How did you know?"

"You had that faraway look in your eyes," he said, smiling. "And I am an expert on women and their faraway looks. Do you miss him very much?"

"I haven't been away long enough to miss him yet," I said. "But I guess I will. We've been together for a whole year."

"In which case it is time for a change," Carlo said, giving me a teasing look. Then he laughed. "Don't worry—I will not try to make you forget him. What is his name?"

"It's Craig."

"Ah, Craig. That sounds like a name for a cowboy. Is he a cowboy?"

"I'm afraid not," I said, laughing, too. "I don't think he's ever ridden a horse in his life."

"No matter. I will not try to make you forget Craig and fall hopelessly in love with me—even if you are the prettiest girl I have seen in a whole year in Paris and even if I think that I fell in love with you the moment I saw you running toward me."

"Let's walk on," I said. "The wind is cold standing here."

Carlo's lighthearted mood seemed to have vanished. We walked side by side, a few inches apart, but not touching.

Craig, I kept saying to myself. *Think of Craig up there in Alaska, shivering in the snow and ice, fighting off wolves.*

Couples strolled past us, arms wrapped around each other. One girl paused to lift her face for a kiss.

"Maybe we should be getting back," I said. "We have to catch a train in the morning."

"Ah, yes," Carlo said. "The boyfriend of Toni waits for her. Do you think that maybe you will be in the way there? Perhaps it would be better to stay on in Paris and leave the young lovers alone?"

"Toni is not the sort of girl you leave alone," I said. "Besides, I don't think I would dare stay in Paris by myself."

"But I would take good care of you."

"That's what I'm afraid of," I said, smiling at him.

"You do not trust me?" he asked, pretending to look horrified.

I was very conscious of his face, a few inches from mine, of those dark eyes gazing down at me. Even though he still had not touched me, it was as if a powerful electric current flowed between us.

"No, Carlo," I answered seriously. "I'm not sure that I trust *me.*"

"Ah," he said, and we walked on in silence.

Before us the lights of a busy intersection flashed across a bridge and danced up from the water. A few more steps and the city awaited us.

"Jeel," he said, laying his hand gently on my arm, "may I ask you one thing?"

"That depends on what it is," I answered.

"I wanted to ask if I could kiss you once before we go back to the busy street."

"I don't think there would be any point, Carlo," I said in a voice I couldn't quite control. "Since I'll never see you again after tonight."

"May I not come and see you at the station tomorrow morning?"

"No, Carlo."

"You are a cruel person," he said, but he managed to smile. "And you will not come and visit me in Venice? I shall be there in about ten more days, and I should love to show you my city. It is so much more romantic than Paris. We could ride together in a gondola, and the bridges and palaces would glide past above our heads while the gondolier sang us a love song. Does that not sound much better than sitting around on a farm while Toni and her French boyfriend want to be alone together?"

"Yes," I said, sighing. "It does sound much better. But it wouldn't work, Carlo. I've had a wonderful evening with you, but I'm glad it's ending now. I don't want things to get more complicated. I have a boyfriend at home, and I'm just in Europe to keep an eye on Toni. I'm going to see the Louvre and the French countryside and go home with my heart in one piece."

He looked at me seriously and nodded. "If that's what you want, Jeel. Then I must say goodbye. I hope you have a wonderful life before you."

"And I hope you don't have to work in the glass factory."

"Maybe we shall meet again someday," he said. "I shall always keep hoping. After all, it was fate that brought us together this morning. I cannot believe that fate wanted us to be parted so soon. And so I do not say goodbye, Jeel. I say *arrivederci*, which means until we meet again. See, here is your Metro station. Safe journey."

His hand brushed mine in a quick caress, then he turned and hurried away. I traveled back to the hotel in a daze.

I'm glad that's the way it ended, I kept telling myself. *I'm glad I didn't let him kiss me. I could've spoiled my whole trip by thinking about him and hoping I'd see him again. Now I just have to concentrate on seeing the sights and getting Toni home safely.*

If everything turned out so well and you're feeling so glad, a voice nagged inside my head, *how come you keep wanting to cry?*

Chapter Eight

"So, did you manage to fight off your sexy Italian?" Toni asked as I crept into the room. "Or didn't you want to fight him off?"

"I thought you'd be asleep by now," I said. "And, for your information, I didn't have to fight him off. He behaved like a perfect gentleman all evening."

"How boring," Toni said. "I could've sworn the way he looked at you this morning that you'd have ended up in a wrestling match this evening."

"I don't want to talk about it, Toni, OK?" I said wearily, sitting down on my bed and taking off one shoe.

"So you didn't have a good time?" she asked suspiciously.

"Yes, I had a wonderful time. He's a terrific person, and I enjoyed every minute, but there's no sense in talking about it because I'm never going to see him again."

"Jill, you don't have to come with me if you don't want to," Toni said after a pause. "I know I made a fuss about not being able to get around on my own. Well, I really think I could if I had to—and I wouldn't want to spoil—"

"Not another one," I snapped. "Carlo has spent half the evening trying to persuade me to stay. Has everyone around me suddenly joined the anti-Craig league? I am perfectly happy with my boyfriend at home. I have no wish to get involved with someone in Europe. Carlo was very nice and very charming as a date for one evening, but that one evening is now over. So let's all forget about it. Do I make myself clear?"

"Very clear," Toni said. "OK. We won't talk about it anymore. But you want to hear something funny?"

"Sure," I said. "Something funny would be a good idea right now."

"Well, we completely misjudged the man downstairs."

"You mean the grouch?" I asked.

"Yes—he's not really a grouch at all. He was very friendly to me this evening. A bit too friendly, actually."

"Why? What happened?" I asked suspiciously.

"I think it was because I tried out my French

66

on him," Toni went on, smiling. "Perhaps that softened his hard old heart. I felt much better, so I went out to McDonald's, and as I came back in I said a couple of sentences in French, and you should have seen him. He came around the corner and put his arm around my shoulder and escorted me to the elevator. I had to give him a good push to stop him from coming in with me."

"Toni," I asked, even more suspiciously, "what exactly did you say?"

Toni shrugged her shoulders. "All I said was that I was feeling hot this evening. I said, '*Je suis très chaud ce soir.*' "

I started to laugh.

"What's the matter," she snapped. "Wasn't my French correct?"

"Not exactly," I spluttered. "What you actually said was 'I'm hot stuff this evening.' "

Toni's eyes opened very wide. "Did I say that? How terrible." Then she started to laugh, too. "Oh, Jill. What a dummy I am. No wonder he was suddenly so friendly. No wonder he looked so disappointed when I slammed the elevator door in his face. Thank heavens we're leaving in the morning. I don't dare look him in the eye again."

We both lay back on our beds, helpless with laughter.

"Jill," Toni said at last, "I'm glad you're coming with me after all. Who knows what terrible trouble I could get myself into without you!"

Chapter Nine

Next morning the sky was gray again. The city below us was half hidden in a wet mist. I didn't mind it. It matched my mood perfectly.

Why can't I be like Toni? I thought. *Nothing ever upsets her for long. She just sort of glides over the surface of life. She falls madly in love for a couple of weeks at a time, then falls out of love again just as easily. And she always comes away with her heart in one piece. Why can't I learn not to get so serious about things?*

But that day, it appeared, was not one of her gliding-over-the-surface days. Toni was decidedly jumpy. She changed her mind about her outfit to meet Philippe in about twenty times. By the time she had decided on white capri pants with a red stripe on the side, a wide-sleeved red cotton blouse, and red mesh belt, every item of clothing that she owned was lying all over our floor, and her suitcase was totally empty.

"Toni!" I exclaimed as I came back from the bathroom. "It took us days to get that case shut in the first place. We'll never get it packed in time to make the train."

"I thought I might pack it while you went to make the phone call," Toni said, not looking up.

"Me make the phone call?" I asked. "Come on, be reasonable—Philippe is *your* boyfriend. Why on earth would he want a phone call from me? I should think the last thing he'd want to hear is that I'm coming to stay."

"But my French is so bad," Toni said, giving me her helpless look. "You know what happened when I tried to speak it last night. Heaven knows what I might say to the operator or to Philippe's father."

"I'll write out an opening sentence for you," I said. "It will just say, 'May I please speak to Philippe.' And you'd better phone him right now, or he'll have gone out to milk the pigs or whatever he does on his farm."

"I guess so," she said, not making any attempt to head for the door. "I've been thinking, Jill. It might be so much better just to arrive—sort of a nice surprise. I mean, if he didn't really want me to come, not one hundred percent, then he could say it wasn't a good time on the phone. But if I was actually there, standing on his doorstep, he couldn't send me back to Paris, could he?"

"But he invited you, you idiot," I said. "You don't invite people unless you want them to come, especially not all the way to France."

I had started this European trip with a lot of uncomfortable feelings. Now I was feeling more and more uneasy. Why was Toni putting off the phone call again?

"I'll phone him from the station," Toni said, grabbing a handful of clothes from the floor and cramming them into her suitcase in a way that made me wince.

"You'd better be a bit more careful," I said. "I don't think the crumpled look is in this year. And from what I remember of Philippe, he cares a lot about the way he looks."

"I never could get the hang of packing," Toni said. "Is this the way you're supposed to fold jeans?"

I couldn't stand it any longer. Between her resistance to calling and her careless packing, I was beginning to prickle. I leaped up and started folding things for her, which was, of course, just what she wanted.

"There," she said as we finally closed the case by means of my sitting on it and bouncing while Toni snapped it shut, "that's done." And she managed to give the impression that she'd done all the hard work herself.

I laughed and shook my head. "You're a con artist, Toni Redmond," I said.

"I hope so," she said, suddenly looking worried.

"Is anything wrong?" I asked.

"Wrong? No. Nothing's wrong. Everything's going to be wonderful," she said, much too brightly. "Today I get to see Philippe again, and everything will be wonderful."

I studied her back as we dragged our suitcases toward the elevator. I never trusted Toni in her much-too-bright moods. I had a feeling that some sort of surprise lay ahead. And not necessarily one I'd like.

We got a taxi to the station, then I steered Toni to the nearest phone booth.

"Get in there," I said. "The train leaves in ten minutes."

"You want me to change into Superman?" she quipped.

"You know what I want you to do," I said. "Here is the piece of paper. Now phone."

She tried. I was there, I watched her, so I know that she really did try. But French phones aren't as automatic as ours. She got an operator a couple of times, gave the name of the town, waited, and then the line went dead. Finally we had to give it up and sprint for our train. As we pulled out of Paris, I was full of uneasy feelings. I worried about arriving at a strange farmhouse when nobody knew we were coming. I also couldn't help thinking about the night before. It wasn't until I was lying in bed, thinking things over, that I realized I didn't even know Carlo's last name. Now I had no chance of ever seeing him again, even if I changed my mind, or even if I ever got to Venice, which wasn't too likely.

For once in her life, Toni was silent, too. We both stared out the windows, watching gray buildings slip past us. We had seen the glamorous side of the city, but that day we saw the not so nice side—dark alleys and crumbling walls with hopeful bright signs painted on them telling everyone to drink Dubonnet. The Dubonnet signs were the only splashes of color in gray streets. We plunged into a tunnel, and both of us gasped and grabbed each other.

"I've just realized this is the first time I've ever traveled on a train," Toni said as we came out into the daylight again.

"Me, too," I said. "Except for the kiddie train in a park somewhere."

"It's really true," Toni said. "They really do go *boddleydee-boddleydoo*. I think I like it." And she gave me a real Toni grin. Then she leaned toward me. "Jill," she said in a low voice, "what if—no forget it."

"What if what?" I asked.

"It doesn't matter. Forget it. Yucky day, isn't it. I'm glad we're not climbing the Eiffel Tower, we wouldn't see a thing today."

"And the poor people below wouldn't be able to see flying purses," I said, then wished I hadn't.

"Do you think you'll write to him ever?" Toni asked, studying my face. "Carlo, I mean."

"No," I said. "I don't even know his last name."

Toni gave a big sigh. "Jill Gardner, you really are a hopeless person," she said. "I can't imagine letting a guy like that disappear without knowing his last name!"

"Yes, well, I'm not like you," I said. "I can only handle one boy at a time. I can hardly run off with the first cute guy I meet just because Craig is up among the Eskimos, can I?"

"I just didn't want you to get bored, that's all," Toni said. "Oh, look, the sun's coming out!"

As she spoke we left the last straggles of the city behind us, the mist swirled and parted, and a watery sun shone down on the French countryside. On one side of us strands of mist clung to willow trees along the banks of a canal. A brightly painted barge was moored to the bank, and two children waved like crazy as the train passed them. Beyond the river a road, straight, dusty, and lined with poplar trees, disappeared into the distance. A lone hay wagon, pulled by a huge horse, moved along it. We passed neat fields, divided by hedges, then a village of houses with tiled roofs and bright awnings.

"I'm glad it looks the way it's supposed to," Toni said with a sigh of satisfaction. "I had a horrible feeling it might be all shopping malls and freeways. It would've been awful to come to Europe and find it was just like home."

"I didn't think the scenery mattered to you," I said. "I thought you'd only have eyes for Philippe."

"I wish you'd stop talking about him," Toni said sharply. "You're making me nervous."

It took a lot to make Toni nervous. As she looked out the window, I studied her with interest. Could it be that she'd come to her senses about Philippe? I didn't know what to say that would make her feel better. After all, this was not the time to tell her I knew all along she was making a mistake with him and she'd be far better off back in Seattle with good old Rich. We'd be arriving at Philippe's house in less than an hour. Also, and no less important, we didn't have enough money between us to bum around Europe until our charter went home in a month. No, like it or not, Toni would now have to make the best of Philippe for a while. I only hoped she'd like it. Toni was not an easy person to be with when she was in a foul temper!

The train stopped at one or two little stations. They were all the same—one platform, a yellow-painted building with peeling shutters beside it, and tubs of geraniums along the fence. Since we didn't know when our station was coming up, we sat perched on the edges of our seats, ready to make a quick getaway, our baggage already in the aisle.

At last Toni screamed, "This is it!" and we flung ourselves at the doors as they began to close. Toni, with superhuman strength, wrenched them open, and we tumbled out. As it turned out, we didn't have to hurry. A dusty, tired-looking man with a droopy mustache shuffled across to have a word with the conductor. They were still talking as we went through the white gate and got out into the tree-lined street beyond.

"Welcome to Vincennes, fun capital of the south," Toni said in her much-too-bright voice. "Where is everybody?"

"Perhaps they've been wiped out by a mysterious plague or been kidnapped by aliens," I said. "Are you going to phone from the station?"

"I have a thing about French phones," Toni said. "They just won't work for me. Why don't we leave our baggage and walk."

"OK," I said doubtfully, not fully trusting the man with the droopy mustache to look after all my worldly goods.

The man shut our bags in a very dusty room and pointed and waved his arms a lot when we asked for directions to the Moreau place.

"Well, at least he's heard of it," I said as we came out into the bright sunlight. "That proves Philippe really does live here. I was beginning to have my doubts."

"This doesn't seem to be in the direction of the village," Toni said, looking around. "I think I see smoke from a chimney over there. I hope he doesn't live too far out of town."

"From what we've seen so far, I shouldn't think there's much night life to be missed," I said. "Maybe the odd folk dance on saints' days and the occasional witch burning—apart from that not too much."

"Maybe Philippe will have some fun friends, and they'll all have fast cars and whiz us down to the nearest city," Toni said. "Didn't the man say it was on this street? It looks like the street turns into a trail down here. I don't see a farm, do you?"

We continued to walk for a short distance, and I said, "Maybe behind that brick wall over there?"

A man passed us on a bicycle, ringing his bell and looking very interested in the two of us. I asked for directions from him. He grinned like an idiot and pointed across the road. "Château Moreau," he said and rode off, giggling.

"Obviously the village idiot," Toni said. "But you must have been right about the brick wall. There must be a gate in it somewhere."

We followed the wall until it turned the corner. Around the corner was a circle of green grass, the wall curved into a semicircle, and in the middle of it was an enormous gateway. The posts were crowned with marble lions, and the gate itself was black iron, tipped with gold. It was also shut. Toni and I tiptoed up to it and peered in.

Beyond the iron-grilled gate a long gravel drive led to an enormous house—the sort you see only in European car commercials. Neat green lawns and flower beds in geometric shapes spread out in all directions. There was even a fountain, although it wasn't gushing right then.

"This can't be it," I said in a whisper.

Toni shrugged her shoulders.

"Did he ever mention living in a castle?" I asked.

"He did sort of," Toni said. "But I didn't quite believe him. You know how he was—"

"But this is incredible!" I exclaimed. "They must be stinking rich. He's probably a prince or something. Won't they be surprised to see two scruffy American girls?"

Toni's face had gone very white. "Jill, I'm scared," she said. "I don't want to go in there."

"After you dragged me all this way across the world?" I said. "I'm not turning right around and going home now. At the very least I want a meal and a shower."

"But I don't think we'll feel right in there," Toni said. "Look at us—"

"Oh, come on, Toni," I said, feeling scared myself but not wanting to admit it. "Philippe knows how you look. Why do you think he invited you if he doesn't want to see you again? He could just have said goodbye at the airport and left it at that."

"Well—" Toni said, looking down at her shoe and drawing a picture in the dust.

A horrible, cold feeling crept over me. She must have had a good reason for pretending she had written to him, for not wanting to phone him, and the only good reason that I could think of was—

"Toni," I said coolly. "He did invite you, didn't he?"

"Well—" she said. "Sure—I mean—"

"What were his exact words?" I demanded, boring into her with an icy stare.

"He said I must look him up if I was ever in Europe—or something like that. I don't remember the exact words."

"Toni," I said, "you have played a very dirty trick on me. You've dragged me to Europe when all I wanted to do was stay home. You let me think that we had a definite invitation. And now it turns out that the guy was just being polite—come and see me sometime. Everyone says things like that. People don't mean it usually. You have done some pretty stupid things in your life, Toni Redmond, but this is the stupidest thing of all."

She didn't even argue. She didn't say anything. She just continued to stare down at her sneakers and draw circles in the dust. "You're right," she said at last. "I've really blown it this time, haven't I?"

I don't know how long we stood in the hot sun

outside the gate. We must have made an interesting picture—two orphans standing outside the king's palace. Neither of us spoke because neither of us could think of anything sensible to say. I was trying to decide whether I felt more angry or scared. Toni was probably trying to decide how she could bluff her way out of this mistake. She didn't like to admit she was wrong, ever. By the end of the day she'd probably have invented a story in which I insisted on dragging her around Europe and convinced her that Philippe wanted to see her again.

A large bee buzzed around us, waking both of us from our thoughts.

"So what do you propose we do now?" I asked.

Toni wouldn't look at me. She was staring into the distance as if she were seeing visions. "I don't know," she said.

"Well, we can't stand here until we die of heatstroke," I said. "I still think we should go on in. Philippe will probably be delighted to see you, and everything will be OK."

"I guess so," she said hesitantly.

"And just think what we can tell the kids at home if we spend the whole summer in a French château!"

"I guess so," she said again.

"After all, you did look after him in the States, didn't you? And you did drive him to the airport, and he did give you a fond farewell—"

"I know," she said. "But it was all different at

home. I didn't know he lived in this sort of house then. I'd be scared to death that I'd break something in a house like this."

The bee had returned again and was buzzing hopefully around my nose. I knocked it away. The anger inside me was winning out over the fright.

"You keep finding a million excuses," I snapped. "Why don't you come right out and say that you don't really want to meet him again. Admit that you made a mistake and you never really cared about him at all, because that's what it sounds like to me!"

"You know that's not true," Toni snapped back, suddenly springing back to life. "I was crazy about him. You know that! And I do want to see him again. I just can't get up the nerve to go in through those gates. I bet they have attack-trained killer dogs roaming around in there."

"Well, I don't want to stand around out here all day," I said. "I'm hot and tired and hungry, too."

"Why don't you go in then," Toni said. "And if you don't get eaten by the time you reach the front door, I'll come in, too."

"So generous of you," I said. "Since Philippe probably won't even remember who I am, he'll let the dogs tear me to pieces."

At this moment there was the sound of tires scrunching over gravel, and a girl on a bicycle came down the road toward us.

"We may be in luck," Toni said, her whole face

brightening up. "She looks like she's coming here. We can send a message to Philippe with her. Or watch her get eaten by the dogs."

The girl was wearing a white lace blouse and a full red skirt, which she had cleverly tucked around her as she rode. She got off her bicycle and began to wheel it across the gravel. Tossing back her long, black hair, she looked at us with interest, mingled with a bit of hesitation. Then she called out something in French, which neither of us understood.

"Is this the house of Philippe Moreau?" I asked as she got off her bike and went up to the gate.

She turned back and looked at us with more interest. "Yes," she said. "And I think you must be friends that Philippe met in America, am I right?"

"Yes, we are," I said, feeling hopeful for the first time.

"How very nice," she said in English, smiling at us warmly. "He had such a good time there. He has told me everything about it. I should like to go and visit America myself one day. Then I could improve my bad English."

"Your English sounds terrific to me," Toni said. She had suddenly turned back into her old self again, bouncy and confident and excited. "But then Philippe told me how hard you have to study in school here. Is he at home right now?"

"I think he is out with his father in the fields,"

the girl said. "But please come in and wait. I know that Philippe will be most pleased to have a visit from American school friends."

She laid her bike down and lifted the latch on the big gate. It swung open with a loud creak.

"Please come in," she said.

"Are you Philippe's sister?" Toni asked. "I thought you were much younger by the way he spoke about you."

The girl threw back her head and laughed, "No, I am not Giselle," she said. "I am Brigitte, Philippe's fiancée."

"Fiancée?" Toni and I both said together.

The girl looked worried. "You do not understand?" she asked. "I wanted to say that Philippe and I will be married."

"Oh, yes," Toni said. "We understood that very well."

"And Philippe has spoken much about me when he was in America?" she asked.

"Not too often," Toni said.

"But why do we stand here in the hot sun?" the girl said, laughing. "Please follow me to the house. Philippe will arrive later, and he will be so surprised!"

"I can imagine," I muttered to Toni. The girl walked ahead. I hung back, waiting to take my cue from Toni to see what she'd do next. I didn't think that even she would have the nerve to walk into the house with Philippe's fiancée.

"I've just remembered," Toni called after her.

"We really don't have time to hang around all day. We were just passing through on our way south. All our baggage is at the station, and we have to catch a train this afternoon. We can't risk missing it, you see. We have reserved seats and everything. So please tell Philippe that a couple of old friends dropped in to say hi, and that we were sorry we missed him. Oh, my goodness, look at the time. We'd better be getting back to the station right now, Jill. Nice meeting you, Brigitte." The words poured out in a torrent, and I don't think Brigitte understood half of them. But Toni was magnificent—bright and cheerful and bouncy as ever. As soon as she had finished talking, she turned and strode away, leaving me to follow after her.

I didn't catch up with her until she'd turned the corner and was on the street leading to the station again.

"You were terrific, Toni," I said. "A truly great performance. Well, thank heavens, we met her before we went in. Can you imagine how embarrassing it would've been if we'd shown up on the doorstep! Honestly, Toni Redmond, you do pick 'em, don't you? I tell you what—next time you decide to fall madly in love with a boy, give me all the details, and I'll run them through my computer so I can tell you if he's suitable or not. That way I won't be dragged into any more embarrassing scenes halfway across the world."

"Can't you ever shut up!" Toni yelled suddenly. She turned on me, her eyes flashing fire, her face scarlet. "You've done nothing but tell me how I've wrecked your summer and how wonderful you are to come with me. Well, I didn't think too much of your summer at home, either. If you really prefer wiping kids' noses in boring, wet old Seattle to meeting a gorgeous guy and strolling around Paris with him, then you need your head examined. Especially when your dear, wonderful boyfriend is off doing goodness-knows-what up in Alaska! So quit bugging me. If you don't enjoy my company, you can go off on your own right now. Because I find you one big, self-righteous pain in the neck!"

"If that's the way you feel, I will," I yelled back. "I know you've never been one bit grateful for anything I've done for you. It doesn't even matter to you that I've spent part of my money for a car to come here with you—and what for? For nothing, that's what—except maybe to go through an embarrassing scene and to end up feeling like a total fool!"

"So go back home and miss out on Europe," Toni shouted. "It's wasted on you anyway. All you're ever going to be is a boring old housewife making peanut butter sandwiches and driving little kids around!"

"But at least I have a boyfriend I'm sure of," I said. "Which is more than you can say, isn't it? At least he's not engaged to anyone else behind my back!"

"Drop dead!" she screamed. "And get out of my sight. I never want to see you or speak to you again."

She stalked ahead of me to the station. Then she had to wait for me because I had the tags for our bags.

"And where do you intend to go now?" I asked as she dragged her enormous suitcase out onto the platform.

"The opposite direction from you," she said icily.

"I'm going back to Paris," I said.

I walked through, into the booking office. "What time is the next train to Paris?" I asked in my best French.

"Eight-twenty-five in the morning," the man with the droopy mustache, who was also the booking clerk, said. He looked very interested, as if he wanted to know more about these two strange girls who arrived, gave him their luggage for an hour, and then came back again.

"But what about this afternoon?" I asked.

"No train until tomorrow," he said.

"Then which train goes south today?"

"No train until tomorrow."

It finally sunk in. "You mean that no train goes from this station until tomorrow morning?" I asked.

He nodded as if he were dealing with an imbecile.

"Oh," I said. I turned and wandered back out

to Toni. She was sitting on the platform between two geranium pots, resting her back against her suitcase and frowning as she stared out into space.

"There's no train until tomorrow," I said, sitting down beside her.

She went on staring. "What about for me?" she asked.

"Not for you either," I said. "It looks like we're stuck here. We'd better find out if there's a hotel or something in the village."

"I'm not spending a night in the same village as that no-good, squirmy little French worm," Toni said through clenched teeth. "I'd rather die than meet him again."

"I think you had a lucky escape," I said. "Now that we know the sort of person he is. Just think how terrible it would've been if you'd gotten yourself more involved with him. Now we can actually get on with enjoying Europe."

"You talk about him as if he's something I can put away like last year's fashion. Did it ever occur to you that I was really crazy about him?"

As she spoke two large tears squeezed themselves out of her eyes and ran down her cheeks. Suddenly she gave a huge sob and buried her face in her hands. She cried and cried, her whole body shaking with each sob. I sat there beside her, feeling scared and sick and not knowing what to do. As I said before, I don't ever remember seeing Toni cry. I began to feel worse and worse. I thought how I'd feel if I'd been looking forward to seeing Craig again and found that he had another girl. My mind played back all the mean things I'd said to Toni. I'd teased her and made her feel even worse, partly because I was feeling scared and angry myself and partly because I never dreamed that Philippe was any different from the other boys on whom Toni had had sudden, short, and dramatic crushes. I'd never thought for a moment that she really cared about him. But now, as I looked back on it, I could see all the signs: she'd been nervous, which was not typically Toni; she hadn't wanted to talk about him, which was also not typical; and she'd been furiously angry afterward, which was usually her way of trying to conceal the fact that something had upset her badly.

"It's OK," I whispered, putting my arm around her. "I know how you must be feeling, but everything will be OK."

"Oh, Jill," she said after her sobs had subsided to small hiccups. "It was so terrible. Like having a nightmare and not being able to wake up. I had no idea. I really, honestly thought he wanted to see me again—the way he kissed me goodbye—he really seemed as if—"

"Here," I said. "Blow for Mama." I produced a box of tissues, took out several, and held them up to her nose. "See, at least my boring old five-year-olds have taught me one useful thing."

She managed a watery smile. "Thanks," she

said. She got through half the box before she had wiped away the last tear. "Jill," she said at last, "I said some terrible things to you. I'm sorry. I was so upset I didn't know what I was saying. I just wanted to strike out at somebody!"

"I understand," I said. "I said some pretty mean things, too. I guess I was angry at you for making me feel scared and embarrassed. But I had no idea how you really felt about Philippe, or I wouldn't have gone on about it. Usually you fall in and out of love so easily and it doesn't seem to mean much to you."

"Only because I manage to hide what I'm feeling better than you," she said. "There have been times when my heart has been broken, too, you know. I just didn't want people to know about it. I hate people feeling sorry for me."

"Oh, Toni," I said, shaking my head. "We've been best friends for years, and we still don't know everything about each other. I'm really sorry about Philippe, and I won't say anything dumb like 'it's all for the best' because I know if anything happened between Craig and me I wouldn't want some stupid person telling me I was lucky. All I can say is that you're pretty tough. You'll get over him."

"But I don't feel tough right now," she said, staring hopelessly across the train tracks. "I don't feel as if I'll ever be able to face anything, ever again. What are we going to do next? I feel like I just want to crawl up among the geraniums and die."

"Oh, Toni," I said. "Come on—you've survived worse than this. Remember when you were that maid last summer, and you spilled the sauce and burned the guy's shirts?"

She nodded. "Seems like I've done one dumb thing after another all my life," she said. "I don't know why you put up with me!"

"Because we make a great team," I said. "Remember how we fought our way out of that car when we went on that blind date? We were pretty gutsy then, weren't we?"

"They were another couple of creeps," she said. "I'm beginning to think all boys are creeps."

"Not all boys," I said. "And you know it. It's just that life has ups and downs, and this definitely counts as one of the downs! But you've bounced back from bigger downs than this."

"Like when I collided with the hamburgers?" she said, sitting up and brushing back her hair. "I can just see those strawberry shakes flying through the air!"

"And the french fries raining down!" I added. We looked at each other and started to laugh.

"Oh, Jill," she said, "I'm glad I talked you into coming with me. I don't think I'd have made it without you."

"Well, it's all behind us now," I said. "We'll pretend that today never existed!"

"You're right," she said, smiling bravely. "And now we can have a great time seeing Europe. We'll go to all sorts of places. Much better than being stuck in this dump for a month."

"There's just one thing," I said, remembering suddenly. "How do we finance this grand tour? If I'm not mistaken, we calculated we had just enough money to get by, provided we stayed with Philippe for most of the month."

"Oh," Toni said, "you're right. Do you think we could wire home for more?"

"I really don't want to do that, Toni," I said. "It would worry our folks too much."

"But we need to find somewhere to spend tonight. I really don't want to run into Philippe at the village inn."

"Maybe there's a bus we could take to the next village or something," I said. "Why don't I go ask the stationmaster."

We walked back through the waiting room and found him outside, raking the gravel into neat circles.

While I was still forming the French sentences in my mind, an old truck screeched to a halt beside the station. A fat, balding man climbed out, looked at us, and scowled.

"You the American girls?" he asked in heavily accented English.

We nodded, too surprised to speak.

"You're very late," he said, puffing angrily. "I come here twice already today. I told you early train, no? Climb in the truck at once so we can get going!"

And as Toni and I stared at each other, he grabbed our suitcases and swung them up into the back of the truck.

Chapter Ten

For the second time in one day, Toni and I just stood still with our mouths open. First a castle had appeared when we are expecting a farm, and then a strange man, wearing a dirty and torn undershirt over a barrel-shaped, hairy chest, started to yell at us and throw our bags into a truck.

The man turned to look at us standing like statues. His fat, ugly face broke into an enormous scowl so that he looked just like a bulldog.

"Come on, come on, don't just stand there. You think this is my only job, meeting girls at station?"

Toni was usually the one who had smart answers and was afraid of nothing. That day, however, she'd had her emotions stretched to the breaking point.

"Do you think he's an escaped lunatic?" she whispered to me. "Do you think we could call the police before he drives off with our luggage?"

I took a deep breath and stepped forward. I could feel my knees trembling inside my jeans.

"I think you must have made a mistake," I said. "I don't know which girls you're waiting for, but we just came here to visit a friend."

The bulldog scowl vanished, and his flabby jaw dropped open. "You are not the American girls I spoke to on the phone last night?" he asked. "The ones who come from Nice to work in my winery?"

"No," I said. "We came from Paris this morning."

"Mon Dieu!" he said, striking himself on the head and managing a weak smile. "A thousand pardons. You must think that I am a little—how you say it—ga-ga." And he pointed to his forehead. "These girls say that they come today, you see. I come to the station to meet each train, but no girls. I think they change their minds and decide they do not want to work when they can be on the beach. Too bad." He walked around to the back of his truck and picked up my suitcase. Then suddenly he swung back toward us, his face now in a big, flabby grin.

"I have a good idea," he said. "How about you come to work for me—my charming, young

93

American ladies? Is not hard work, picking the grapes. Much fun. Lots of other young peoples from all over the world and good food and wine. And you make good money, too. You come and try. See if you like."

"How about it?" I murmured to Toni.

"Well, it does seem like a miracle," she said. "Almost too good to be true."

"So shall we take it?" I asked cautiously.

"I'm not too excited about old rubber face over there," she said. "I can just see him walking around with a whip. But we do need somewhere to go and some way to earn money—"

"And maybe we could earn enough in a couple of weeks to have another couple of weeks seeing Europe properly."

"Yeah," she said, her face lighting up. "OK. Let's do it."

She walked over to the truck. "OK, mister, you got yourself two workers," she said, climbing up into the back of the truck. I climbed in after her, not quite so eagerly, and the truck screeched away, leaving a screen of dust behind it.

"I hope we're not doing anything stupid," I said, clinging tightly to the side of the truck.

"I tell you what," Toni said. "If we get there and we don't like the look of things, we just don't stay. We're safe so far. There are two of us and only one of him."

"I guess so," I said. "But you know me—I'm cautious by nature. I wouldn't take a ride in a strange truck at home. And now we're disappearing into the middle of France, and nobody would even know where we were if something happened to us."

"The station man saw us go," Toni said.

But that didn't make me feel any better. I spent the rest of the journey trying to reassure myself.

Soon the truck turned off the paved road and bumped along a dusty road between endless fields of grapes. Toni and I coughed and spluttered in the back of the truck as the dust rose up in a fine yellow cloud behind us. It seemed like hours before we finally lurched to a halt beside some long, long wooden huts. Still spluttering, we climbed down.

"This reminds me of something," Toni said, surveying the two wooden buildings.

" 'Hogan's Heroes' maybe?" I asked.

Toni grinned. "Even worse than that. The summer camp I went to when I was nine. It had the same horrible huts, and all the roofs leaked, and it rained on my bed every night, and we had macaroni and cheese every night for dinner—and you know how I feel about macaroni and cheese!"

"Well, at least it's not going to rain on us here," I said. "Everything looks so dusty I bet it hasn't rained in months. And I bet the French don't cook macaroni and cheese either."

Our fat friend had climbed down from the cab

and was busy dumping our bags on the dusty road.

"OK," he said, scowling again. "Come on, follow me."

"A true gentleman," Toni muttered as she tried to drag her suitcase after him. "You wait till the whips come out."

"This is girls' sleeping room," the man said, opening a creaking door and showing us a row of iron cots, exactly like a scene out of "Hogan's Heroes."

"You can take empty beds, then come down to office and I show you how we work."

"I notice he didn't mention eating," I said as soon as he had left.

"And this isn't exactly the Ritz," Toni said, looking around the room with a disgusted stare.

"We thought that place in Paris was bad," I said, beginning to laugh.

"And now it seems like luxury," Toni said, laughing, too. "Oh, Jill, why don't you and I ever have normal lives like everyone else?"

"Maybe because we'd find it too boring?" I asked. "Here, take this bed by the window, and I'll have the one in the corner. At least it looks clean. I wonder if the bathroom is worse than the hotel's?"

"I'll go find out," Toni said. "I need it right now."

She soon came back, and her face was very white. "Jill, it's terrible," she said. "There's no actual bathroom. You wash under a pump out-side, and the toilet is just a kind of hole in the ground, but it is inside. I tried to flush it with the bucket of water near it, and you know what? Water started gurgling up, and I couldn't get the door open again! It started rising higher and higher. Honestly, I thought I was going to be the only person in the world ever drowned in a john!"

I tried not to laugh, but I couldn't help it.

"It's not funny," she said angrily. "You'll have to go eventually, and then you'll see for yourself. And that's not all. There's a large black spider sitting right above the door. I didn't dare shake the door to get it open for fear the spider would drop on my head!"

"Poor Toni," I said, grinning. "It hasn't been one of your better days, has it?"

"You can say that again," she said. "In fact I'm thinking of officially declaring it 'tomorrow.' "

Chapter Eleven

I sat down on the hard iron-framed cot and looked around me. Although the room was primitive, like the worst sort of summer camp, at least there weren't any visible spider webs above my bed, and I could see a wonderful view of the hills melting into the blue distance.

Our fat, scowling friend came looking for us, even before we had time to get any working-in-the-fields clothes unpacked.

"Come on, come on," he yelled through the open window. "I don't have all day to stand about."

"We have to change our clothes first," I called out through the window.

"You'll do just fine as you are," he said.

"These may look like working clothes to you,

but they are our best traveling clothes," Toni chimed in, poking her head out of the window. "And we do not want to ruin them. We'll be out in five minutes."

Then she gave me a small, triumphant grin as she turned away from the window. It really was impossible to keep Toni down for long, I decided as I wriggled into a pair of shorts, crouching in the corner where old flabby cheeks wouldn't be tempted to spy on me.

A few minutes later we were bumping and lurching out across the dry, rutted road to a slope dotted with grape pickers.

"Here, basket," he said, pointing to something almost the size of Toni. "All you do is fill that with grapes. Only ripe grapes, you understand. I don't want to find little green ones. When you're done you take the basket over to this table, and the boy will check it off for you. You get paid for each basket. Make lots of money, no?"

With that he climbed back into his truck and drove off in a cloud of fine white dust. Toni and I stood there, conscious of the sun beating directly down on us and of the screech of cicadas all around—a high, constant whine, like the sound of the heat itself.

"I guess we'd better get started," I said doubtfully.

We started picking. At first it seemed very easy. Just bend over and pick off the little purple bunches and drop them into the basket. Nothing to it. After an hour or so, we weren't so sure. The sun got hotter, and the bunches of grapes grew lower and lower until our backs felt as if they would break. In addition, the vines were full of sharp prickles, and the grapes stained our hands purple.

"Look at me," Toni said, holding up hands covered with scratches and purple blotches. "I look as if I've been wrestling with a tiger!"

"But we've almost got one basket filled," I said. "Here, help me drag it back to the table."

Suddenly a horn sounded, and everybody started to make his or her way back. We joined a long line standing at the table. Everyone looked at us with interest.

"Where did you two come from?" someone asked in French.

"From the United States," I said.

"Oh, American," people said, switching to English. "They must be the two Gaston hired to replace Inge and Heidi."

"You must watch out for Gaston," a tall blond girl said. "Always he tries to be fresh with the new girls. He thinks he is very attractive, I believe."

There was a great roar of laughter.

The teasing and laughter went on all evening. It was strange to suddenly be part of such a loud, lively group. Actually it was louder and livelier than any group I could remember at home. Everybody seemed to speak English, even though there were kids from all parts of Europe. They made us feel very welcome, and in no time at all we were part of the group, trading insults with Swedes and Austrians.

Dinner was huge plates of pasta, lots of salad, and cold cuts of salami and other sausages I'd never eaten before. It all tasted delicious.

"You know what," Toni said as we walked across to our cabin under a new silver sliver of moon, "I think this is going to be fun."

Chapter Twelve

"You know," Toni said, looking up from behind a huge basket of grapes, "I've been thinking—"

"No!" I said, wiping the sweat away from my forehead with the back of my hand. "A miracle!"

Toni gave me her famous Queen Victoria stare. "As I was saying before I was so rudely interrupted," she continued, "I've been thinking. And the conclusion I've come to is that I didn't have to come halfway around the world to pick grapes. I could have driven down to California."

"Ah," I said. "But just think of all the foreign culture you're picking up over here."

"Like what?" Toni asked.

"You now know the French word for 'grape,' " I said.

"I have news for you, Jill Gardner," she said. "I have a perfectly good dictionary at home with the French word for grape in it. A six-thousand-mile journey was not necessary to learn to say *raisin!*"

I laughed. So did Toni. "Honestly, Jill," she said, sinking onto a pile of earth, "haven't you asked yourself more than once during the last week why we're doing this? I mean, when you tell people you're going to Europe, they have visions of sidewalk cafés and palaces and things. We can hardly go home and tell people that all we saw were four rows of grapes!"

I squatted down beside her. "I know what you mean," I said. "I feel as if I'm in a prison camp, and I keep looking for ways out under the wire. But the evenings have been fun, haven't they?"

"They're fun kids, I agree," Toni said. "I like all the singing and eating part of it. Or, at least, I would if I didn't keep falling asleep in the middle of it."

"And don't forget the most important thing," I said, getting to my feet as Gaston's head appeared farther down the hill. "We get paid tomorrow. If we have enough money, we'll split and head for somewhere exotic—like Venice."

The words just slipped out. I hadn't meant to say that at all. Toni gave me an interested sideways look. "Why Venice?" she asked. "I thought Rome was supposed to be much more interesting."

"Venice," I said firmly, "is supposed to be very romantic."

"You have it on the best authority, I gather," Toni said, grinning at me. "But if I remember correctly, you don't even know his last name. Venice is a big place."

I felt my cheeks turning pink. "Who said anything about wanting to meet him again?" I asked. "I just think Venice would be a very spectacular place to go. Wouldn't you like to drift along in a gondola?"

"I guess so," Toni said. "But then at the moment anything to do with water sounds good to me."

"Then you'd better get working fast," I said under my breath. "Because Gaston is heading this way and might decide to withhold your daily ration if you haven't filled that basket yet."

"At least he hasn't tried to grab either of us yet," Toni said, tossing grapes vaguely in the direction of the basket. "I don't know whether that's a good sign or not. Do you think we're both losing our sex appeal?"

"Frankly I have no wish to try out my sex appeal on that repulsive little man," I said. "If he doesn't find me attractive, then that's the best news I could have." I looked up to watch him pant his way up the last few yards toward us.

"Ah, the American girls—they are working hard. That is good," he said, grinning at us to show his mouth full of gold and black teeth. "That is very good. Now the boss will be pleased when he come today. He will say, Gaston, you have trained them well. Especially you, *ma petite*," he added, sidling over to Toni.

Toni gave him a look that would have stopped a cockroach in its tracks, but it didn't seem to worry Gaston. He went right up to her. "But we must not work too hard," he said. "Not good to work when the sun is overhead. Why do we not take a rest in the shade of the tree? See, *ma petite*, you can come and sit with me in the shade, no?"

"No," Toni said icily. "I'm not at all tired, thank you."

"Oh, but the American girls are so strong," Gaston said. He slipped an arm around her shoulders. "Look at this muscle!" He squeezed her arm. I was torn between wanting to laugh or be angry. Toni's face was wonderful. I could tell she was about to explode any minute.

"American girls like to play hard to get," Gaston went on. "But all girls really admire Gaston."

He swung her toward him to lock her in a full embrace, but Toni was too quick and strong.

She pushed him full in his flabby stomach and caught him off balance. He took a step backward and sat heavily in the basket of grapes. The basket rocked, tipped, and began to roll down the hill, so we were treated to the sight of Gaston, bumping and spinning away from us, his bottom firmly wedged in the basket, while purple grapes flew in all directions.

"Wow," I said as he finally came to a halt against a fig tree. "That was truly spectacular. One of your best efforts, I think."

Toni looked at me, her eyes shining. "Somehow I don't think he's going to be very pleased about this," she said. Then we both burst out laughing.

A crowd had gathered at the bottom of the slope, and pickers were busily trying to pull Gaston out of the basket. Gaston's face was an interesting shade of purple.

"That girl," he was yelling. "That idiot girl! She does this! She makes a fool of Gaston! But I show her—nobody make a fool of Gaston. You may leave now, American girls. Pack your bags and go!"

Toni hurried down the hill ahead of me. "Delighted," she said. "We've had enough of this slave labor anyway. But don't forget you owe us a week's wages first!"

"Money!" Gaston roared. "You get no money! You just get out!"

"But you owe us," I joined in. "We've picked grapes for a whole week. You owe us that!"

"That's right, Gaston," other kids joined in. "You owe them what they've earned."

"I say they get nothing," Gaston spluttered. "They make the trouble. If they do not go now, I call the police. They can see how they enjoy France from jail, no?"

I was beginning to feel scared—supposing the police did come and they didn't understand English and they believed Gaston? But Toni was a fighter. She was not the sort of person to give in when her honor was at stake.

"Go ahead," she yelled. "Go call your police. When they come, I'll tell them how you're trying to cheat me out of my money, and I'll also tell them how you tried to grab me and drag me under a tree."

"That's right," I added. "She has a witness, too."

While this was going on, a Jeep had driven up. "Gaston—what's going on here?" a voice called. "What is all this shouting about?"

"Now you're in trouble," Gaston said, gloating at Toni. "Now the boss comes. He will be angry that you make us all stop work and you spill grapes!"

He sauntered over to the Jeep. "This girl," he said, pointing a finger at Toni. "She make much trouble. I am just telling her to get out!"

"That's not true," Toni said, stumbling along

107

in her not-too-marvelous French. "This man was bad to me!"

The boss climbed down from the Jeep, and Toni looked up. "Toni?" he said at the same time she said, "Philippe?"

They both stood there, staring at each other.

"Toni, what are you doing here?" he asked in English.

"I was picking grapes until that horrible creep fired me," Toni said. "What are you doing?"

"But this is my land," Philippe said. "My father owns this countryside." He was smiling down at her delightedly.

"Well, what a coincidence," Toni said. Her voice trembled.

"But why do you pick grapes?" Philippe asked. "Is this not a boring thing to do?"

"Very boring," Toni said. "But we needed some money to tour Europe."

"But you do not need the money. You can stay with me," Philippe said. "My family lives close by. We should be enchanted. Please, come with me now."

I glanced at Toni to take my cue from her. She looked back at me and gave a small shrug of her shoulders.

"I should have thought your house would be much too crowded," she said in an icy voice.

Philippe looked surprised. "But my house, she is not small," he said. "There will be plenty of room for you."

"There might be room," she said. "But I get the feeling I wouldn't be too welcome!"

"Toni!" he said, stepping toward her. "Why should my Toni not be welcome at my house? Please come—I couldn't bear it if you were so close to me and then went away again."

I looked across at her. I could tell she was wavering. She glanced around at Gaston and the fields, then she turned back to Philippe. "Well, why not?" she said, sounding wonderfully casual. "Of course my friend Jill is also with me—you remember Jill, don't you? And we could only stay for a day or so because we have to be in Venice shortly."

"I understand," Philippe said. "You stay as long as you wish. Come, we will find your baggage." He reached out and touched her shoulder. "Toni, it is so good to see you again."

"It's good to see you, too, Philippe," she said, looking up steadily into his eyes.

At this point Gaston asked something in rapid French. Philippe turned and answered him, and it was wonderful to watch the expression on Gaston's face turn to one of alarm.

"Please excuse me," he said to Toni. "I did not know you are friend of Monsieur Moreau. I go now to get the money you have earned."

Toni gave me a quick grin of triumph as we climbed into the Jeep.

"Toni?" I asked in a low voice while Philippe

109

was still giving directions to the other pickers. "Are you sure you can handle this?"

She shrugged her shoulders again. "It sure beats Gaston or jail, doesn't it?" she said as she climbed in beside me.

Chapter Thirteen

A week after we had peered in dismay through those huge iron gates, we had finally arrived at the place where we'd planned to spend our vacation. We didn't go in through the main entrance, but across the fields from the rear. The back of the house didn't seem quite so frightening. It had none of that tidy elegance of the front gardens and was surrounded by sheds and stables. A tractor was parked outside. Washing flapped from a line, and chickens were running around.

But even though the back of the house didn't scare me as much as the front had done, I still felt a tight knot of worry in my stomach. What might happen when Toni was under the same roof as Philippe and his fiancée was anybody's

111

guess. I just prayed it wouldn't all end up in a big, emotional scene.

Philippe didn't look at all worried as he helped us down from the Jeep. He called out something, and a man appeared from the nearest barn. The man hurried toward us, a broad smile on his face, curious interest in his eyes.

"Welcome, welcome," he said in French, lifting our cases from the car. "We are glad to have American visitors to stay."

"Thank you," Toni said, smiling back. She turned to Philippe. "Is that your father?" she asked.

Philippe looked horrified. "That is our head gardener," he said.

"Oh, gee, I'm sorry," Toni muttered, raising an eyebrow as she looked across at me. "I guess we're not used to head gardeners and things back home."

"You'll be able to meet my father at dinner," he said. "Today he is in Paris, I think. My mother and sister, also. But that is good because then I can spend the whole afternoon alone with you." And he gave Toni a special look that made me feel that somehow I wasn't included in the afternoon's plans.

We followed Philippe in through a small side door and along a narrow passageway, which led into a long, wide hall. Philippe opened a set of double doors, and we stepped into an enormous room.

"Wow," Toni muttered under her breath. "It's just like a museum!"

I was glad that she said it because it was just what I was thinking.

"Please sit down," Philippe said. "I will inform the housekeeper that you are here."

As soon as he'd gone, Toni gave me a nervous grin. "Do you feel like we've stepped into the set of some play?" she asked. "I keep expecting those big double doors to open and someone in a long, flowing dress to come sweeping in."

"So long as it's a living person and not a ghost," I said.

"How will you be able to tell the difference?" Toni asked.

"If I can see through it, I'll run," I said, and we both giggled because we were both feeling pretty nervous by this time.

"Jill, what's the matter with us?" Toni asked, suddenly serious. "Other people go on European tours and they stay at normal hotels, see all the things tourists are supposed to see, and then go home again. They don't get kidnapped by grape pickers and taken into spooky old houses."

"But think of the interesting stories we'll be able to tell when we get home," I said. "All other people can do is show pictures of the Eiffel Tower."

"It's a pity we didn't get an action shot of your flying purse," Toni said. "Especially at the moment when it almost hit Carlo. Then at least you'd have had a picture to remember him by."

"Yes," I said, staring out through the french windows and across the neat, manicured lawns.

"Philippe did seem pleased to see me, didn't he?" Toni asked.

"Yes," I said again. "He did."

"So do you think we misunderstood about that fiancée thing?"

"Why would she claim to be his fiancée if she wasn't?" I asked.

"Jealousy. She's madly in love with him, and he tells her all about me and so she tries to drive me away with lies."

I looked at Toni, trying to tell whether she was joking or not. It wasn't always easy to tell if she was putting me on. "Well," she said, noting my skeptical look. "It's a good story isn't it? Look—don't worry, Jill. I don't think I'm involved anymore. I can already think about Philippe without my knees melting, so even if the fiancée thing is true, it doesn't matter. We'll just stay here for a couple of days until we decide where to go next, OK?"

"I always knew you were tough, Toni," I said.

She laughed. "Anyone who can push a tub of lard like Gaston down an entire mountain is no weakling," she said triumphantly. "That was very satisfying, wasn't it?"

I nodded. "Especially when we ended up with

114

our wages, too. Do you realize we have enough money to survive for a few weeks now? We can actually go somewhere."

"Like Venice?" Toni quipped.

"Why not?" I agreed.

After that Philippe returned with a little dumpling of a housekeeper who spoke no English, also no French that I could understand. She beckoned us to follow her up a curved flight of stairs and along another long gallery. Then she led us into another large room, dominated by an enormous carved wooden bed.

"Wow," I said. "We'll need to pole vault to get into bed at night. I've never seen a bed that high."

"I don't like the look of it," Toni muttered. "It's so old. It looks like the sort of bed somebody was murdered in."

"Gee, thanks," I said. "You sure have guaranteed a restful night's sleep for me."

"Well, it does," she said, giggling nervously. "And that closet looks as if something unspeakable was kept in it."

"Oh, Toni, shut up," I said. "It's all right for you. You don't have a vivid imagination like me. I'll lie awake, staring at that closet all night now. When I'm not watching for the door handle to open."

Toni went on giggling while she opened her suitcase and started flinging outfits all over the bed. As soon as we'd washed and changed into something more respectable than grape-picking clothes, we went downstairs again and found Philippe waiting in the front hall.

"Tonee," he said, beaming at her. "You look beautiful. Just as I remembered you. You must let me show you my house and gardens. We have a wonderful rose garden where the roses grow right over the path, and you can walk there and nobody can see you. And the smell of roses—ah, it is so romantic! Come!"

He took Toni's arm very firmly and led her out through the front door, making it quite clear that I was not included in the invitation. As I watched them go, I began to wonder if I dared go to Venice by myself.

But what use would that be, I thought as I walked down the front steps and turned along the gravel path, away from the rose garden. *I've no way of meeting him again, even if I wanted to.*

Toni and Philippe did not show up again until evening. I'd wandered around the house and garden without meeting a soul and had finally gone back to our room, checked out the closet for unspeakable things, and started to write a letter to Craig. But I couldn't find a way to describe all the things that had happened to us without making us sound really dumb and naive. And I wanted Craig to think that I was having a wonderful time and surviving very well without him.

I didn't have time to speak to Toni much before dinner. She had a distant look on her face, as if she wanted to be alone with her thoughts.

"Philippe says that dinner is at eight," she said. "And we get to meet all of his relatives then."

As we entered the dining room, I again felt the sensation of being on a movie set. There was a long table that stretched the length of the room. There were the large, imposing double doors through which we'd entered, but from which we'd not moved an inch. Portraits of long-gone Moreaus lined the walls, their somber faces reflecting the other somber faces that peered up at us from the table.

Toni and I stood frozen, each daring the other to go in first. Then Philippe jumped up and came over to us.

"Mama," he said. "Here are the visitors I told you about. Mademoiselle Toni Redmond and her friend."

"Ah, yes," the mother said, nodding gravely and not looking at all overjoyed to see us. "Please be seated. We are delighted to have school friends of Philippe to visit."

As we walked to our chairs, we could feel ourselves being inspected. But we both managed to sit down without falling over the rug or doing anything terrible. They'd put us near the head of the table beside an empty chair.

"Do you think that's for the family ghost?" Toni whispered. I didn't answer because at that moment I was watching a handle on the double doors. It was turning, very slowly. Then the door opened, very slowly. When the figure in black drifted in, I couldn't help giving a sort of hiccupping scream that made everyone at the table turn and look at me.

Philippe had risen to his feet again. "Grand-mère," he was saying. He walked to meet the figure in black. "Grandmère, we have visitors." He turned to us. "I should like to present my grandmother," he said as he escorted her to the empty chair. At second glance she was just as frightening as when she'd appeared around that door.

She was tall and thin, dressed head to toe in black. Her hair was pulled severely back from her face. She had a hook nose and sunken eyes, so that looking at her was like looking at a skull. From her expression she didn't think we looked much better, either.

"How charming," she said in English. "For what reason do you come to France?" And her expression said, "I know you are chasing my grandson."

"We want to see Europe before we start college," I muttered. She nodded. "Ah, yes, the famous tour of Europe. No?"

Food was brought in and placed in front of us

A salad of green beans, swimming in oil. We tried to make polite conversation while oil from the beans ran down our chins.

"So you helped to keep my grandson occupied in America?" the grandmother asked.

"Oh, yes," I answered before Toni could speak. "Very occupied." I felt Toni kick me under the table and had to stare down hard at my plate in case I started to giggle.

"Philippe never mentioned you in his letters home," his mother said, expertly mopping up her oil with a piece of bread. "We often wondered if the poor boy was lonely."

"I know why he didn't mention them," the little dark girl at the far end of the table said, giving Toni a long stare. "It is because they are more beautiful than Brigitte, and she would have been jealous."

"Hush, child," her mother said, frowning at her.

"But it's true," the girl went on. "This one with the curls I like her, and Philippe does, too! Look at his face!"

"Giselle, this is not suitable conversation for the dinner table," the father said. "Now we will talk of proper subjects only."

"How was your day in Paris, Gregoire?" the grandmother asked, and we sat there, half understanding, while they all described what they had done. Another plate was brought in. Lots of little crispy things.

"These are interesting," Toni said, crunching hard. "What are they?"

"Larks," the grandmother said.

"Larks?" Toni asked. "What is that?"

The grandmother frowned. "Is that not the correct word? Little birds. Tweet, tweet."

Toni shot me a look of horror. "We're eating little birds," she whispered. "I've been crunching bird bones."

"They are a delicacy here," the mother added. "Philippe asked us to prepare a special meal in your honor tonight. I hope you like them."

"Oh, yes," we both managed to mumble. "Delicious."

The next dish was a pastry shell stuffed with a delicious creamy sauce. *At least it doesn't have bones*, I thought as I ate it.

"And what is this?" Toni asked. "This is really delicious."

"Ah," the grandmother said, smiling for the first time as if we'd finally said the right thing. "Another specialty of our house. Calves' brains."

Suddenly the creamy sauce didn't taste nearly so delicious. I noticed Toni was only playing with hers, too. But we both managed to struggle through them, with the help of large gulps of water. Dinner went on until about ten, with course following course. Luckily the other things were identifiable, and we could enjoy them without wondering what we were swallowing.

"That was a wonderful meal," Toni said, flinging her arm expansively and knocking over a water jug. "Oh," she stammered. "I'm sorry." She jumped up and knocked her chair over backward. "Let me get something to wipe it up."

"Mademoiselle," Grandmother said firmly, grabbing at Toni's wrist with her skeletonlike grip. "Calm yourself."

"But your beautiful cloth," Toni said, trying to pick up her chair and mop up the water at the same time. "I'll just run to the kitchen."

"Mademoiselle," the grandmother said even more firmly. "For what reason do we have servants? Please seat yourself. The servants will arrange all."

"I think Toni is tired, Grandmère," Philippe said, noticing Toni's look of panic as the grandmother still clutched at her arm. He got to his feet. "If you will excuse us." And he swept her out of the room. I was left to make more conversation and wonder what was happening upstairs.

At last the grandmother released me, and I staggered up to our room. Toni was already lying in bed, staring at the ceiling.

"Well?" I said bluntly.

"Philippe has just told me that he loves only me," Toni said, still staring at the ceiling.

"Did the small matter of the fiancée come up in the conversation?" I asked.

"Oh, yes," she said. "He told me all about her. He said their marriage was arranged years ago when they were toddlers because their parents wanted to join their two farms together."

"How romantic," I said. "And what does Philippe think about that?"

"He says he'll probably marry her one day," she said. "When he is about thirty. But that he only loves her as a sister, and she doesn't prevent him from a real romance."

"I see," I said.

"He even suggested," she said hesitantly, "that I stay on in France all summer. Then we can be students together in Paris in the fall. Only we'll have to be discreet because he respects Brigitte, and he doesn't want to hurt her feelings."

"How nice of him," I said. "And what do you feel about all this?"

She still stared at the ceiling. "Funny thing," she said. "If he'd told me he loved me a couple of weeks ago, I would've been in heaven." Suddenly she sat up and propped herself up on her elbow. "But now I couldn't care less. I mean, I have no intention of staying in this creepy place one minute longer than I have to. Can you imagine having dinner here every night with Grandmother sitting beside us and our wondering all the time what unspeakable things we're eating?" She started to laugh. "Oh, Jill," she said. "I nearly died—little birds and calves' brains!"

"Oh, Toni," I said, laughing, too. "I'm so glad you want to leave as much as I do. I was terrified you'd want to stay here with Philippe and I'd be left alone all the time."

"I've found out something about Philippe," she said.

"That he's conceited?" I asked.

"Oh, I knew that all the time," she said. "Now that I can see him in his own home, I've found out something else—Philippe is boring! We spent the whole afternoon meeting his ancestors," she added. "Portrait after portrait, this battle and that battle, and me tiptoeing from room to room, trying not to break things. He even took me out to their graveyard, and I had to visit all the graves. I mean, is that a normal boy-girl thing to do?"

I lay back on the bed, laughing. I was laughing so hard that it hurt.

"From now on give me normal, red-blooded American boys," she said. "Even good old Rich seems perfect now. I think I'll write to him. Jill— let's get out of here first thing in the morning."

"Toni," I said, "that's the first sensible thing you've said in months!"

Chapter Fourteen

Neither of us slept much that night. We kept the light on and waited for the closet to open, which luckily it didn't. Next morning we packed and told Philippe we were leaving. He seemed amazed.

"But, Tonee," he said, "you have just arrived. I was looking forward to our beautiful summer together. We would walk together in the moonlight and swim in the lake and take picnics—I cannot let you leave me."

"But, Philippe, we have to go," Toni said. "Jill has an appointment in Venice."

"Then let Jill go alone," he said, pouting like a spoiled little boy. "She does not need you. I need you here."

"Oh, I'm afraid she needs me much more,"

Toni said, looking down at her feet so that she didn't start laughing. "She's a very helpless sort of person. I promised I'd come to Europe to take care of her. If I let her go alone, she'd end up on the wrong train, and she'd speak to strange men. I'm sorry, Philippe, but I'm sure you understand, don't you."

Philippe shot me a look of pure hatred while I tried to look like an idiot who couldn't get on the right train by myself.

"I'm sorry, Jill," Toni said after he had left in a huff. "But I couldn't think of any other excuse to leave in a hurry!"

After that everything passed quickly, as in a dream. We gulped down our coffee, loaded our bags into the car, getting no help at all from Philippe, who was behaving more like a spoiled little boy than ever. He was giving Toni a really hard time, at one moment begging her not to leave him and swearing undying love for her, at the next telling her how mean and selfish she was to go away. I decided that that morning would have convinced Toni to fall out of love with Philippe Moreau if she hadn't already done so.

Then we were politely shaking hands with the family and climbing into the backseat of the Jeep. Nobody looked too upset to see us go, except Philippe—and maybe his little sister. She came over to me as I was settling myself into the backseat.

"My mother is glad you depart," she said confidentially. "She thinks your friend makes the trouble for Brigitte. But I like your friend better. She is more amusing than Brigitte, and she makes me laugh. Do you think your friend would like to marry Philippe?"

"I don't think so," I answered. "In fact, I'm sure of it."

Toni must have been thinking the same thing. As the Jeep started to move away down the gravel drive, she looked back, then turned to me. "I feel sorry for Brigitte," she said.

We approached the iron gates. A little bald man shuffled out of a gatehouse and opened them for us. We turned the corner and drove to the station.

"Another episode in my life bites the dust," Toni said. "I begin to wonder if I'll ever meet the right person for me. They all turn out to be super-creeps."

"Rich isn't a super-creep," I said.

"You're right," she agreed. "Rich was nice. A little too quiet for me, maybe, but definitely nice. I was pretty mean to him, wasn't I? But I couldn't help it. I just fell so crazily in love with Philippe, I couldn't think about anything or anyone else."

"Well, as you say, it's all over now, thank goodness. On with the future!"

"Great idea," Toni said. The Jeep was slowing

down now outside the station. "Where are we going?"

I peered out at the deserted station. "Remembering how many trains come through here each day, I'd say we take the first one in either direction."

She nodded. "I wouldn't mind going back to Paris," she said. "That was fun."

"I wouldn't mind either," I agreed.

"What about Venice?" she asked, giving me a sideways look.

"I've been thinking about that," I said. "And I really don't know. Part of me wants to see Venice, and I guess part of me wants to meet Carlo again. But I know that would be almost impossible—and I really don't know if I want to go through the complications of meeting him again. What I really want is Craig, waiting at the station for me, along with my parents."

"Let's call them up," Toni said. "After all, we should let them know that we aren't staying at Philippe's house after all. And we haven't written since Paris."

I had a sudden vision of the letters from Craig waiting for me at home, of my mother's warm, calm voice reading them to me. "We'll call them up from Paris," I agreed.

I went to ask the same tired-looking man with the mustache about trains. He waved his arms a lot and reeled off a list of names that meant nothing to me until I managed to understand that the train was bound for Geneva, Switzerland.

I went back to Toni. "As far as I can understand," I said, "the only train that is stopping here today goes to about three million places I've never heard of. But if we stay on long enough, it gets into Geneva at eight tonight. How does Switzerland grab you?"

"Anything to get safely far away from here," she said. "Look, here it comes now."

As we pulled out of the station, I could see the little station man staring after us as if he couldn't believe that we'd finally gone.

"I've always wanted to see Switzerland," Toni said as we settled ourselves in the corner seats of an empty carriage. "All those cuckoo clocks and mountains—and it's conveniently on the way to Venice!"

"Will you shut up about Venice," I said. "I will be perfectly happy to spend the next two weeks sitting on a mountain, thinking."

"Sounds boring," Toni said. "I hope you won't mind if I'm off with the friendly local goatherds while you're thinking! I need someone to cheer me up after the disappointment of Philippe."

I looked at her and frowned. "I would have thought, after Philippe and Gaston, you'd never want to get near another European man!"

"Oh, I'm sure there are some nice ones

around, if you look hard enough," she said, grinning mysteriously.

For the next hours we passed through field after field of grapes. In some of them people like us were picking, and we made jokes about Gaston and the spiders in the bathroom. It was strange to realize that we were completely free— that we were heading across Europe and nobody was expecting us and nobody knew where we were going and we could stop off whenever we felt like it. It was an exciting feeling, but scary, too!

We crossed the border to Switzerland after lunch and gazed out of the window at Lake Geneva, shimmering silver and surrounded by white-tipped mountains. The train stopped in Geneva, and we unloaded our bags, feeling lost and scared again. But we were now in efficient Switzerland. We asked the woman at the tourist booth about cheap hotels, and she gave us the name of a student hostel right on the lake. She even showed us how to make a phone call to the States. Toni called first and seemed to take forever, babbling on about France and vineyards and trains, while carefully avoiding any of the stranger things that had happened to us.

"Guess what?" she said as she hung up the phone. "There are letters from Rich, and he stopped by the house one day. Wasn't that sweet of him?"

Then it was my turn. When my mother came on the line, clear and as close as if in the next room, I couldn't stop myself from crying. I felt stupid tears roll down my cheeks, and I fought to keep them out of my voice. She told me about the golf tournament that my father was playing in, and how my sister's kids had both caught colds and missed the picnic. And about snails eating her petunias—just the sort of things she always told me when I came home from school and sat in the kitchen drinking a glass of milk. I couldn't believe she was half a world away. Then she told me about the cat choosing to sleep on my bed all day. "I guess he misses you as much as we do," she said, and I heard the catch in her voice. "Your father has been marking off the days on the calendar until you come home."

Finally I dared to ask the question. "Have there been any letters for me?"

"Oh, a few," she said. "From your college, I think."

"From Craig?"

"Nothing from Craig yet," she said.

"Are you sure?" I asked. "It's been almost two weeks. He promised he'd write."

"I don't suppose there are too many post offices up there in Alaska," my mother said. "And I'm sure he's busy the first couple of weeks."

"Sure," I said. "Too busy to write."

*　　*　　*

That evening we wandered down to the lake. The setting sun had tipped the mountains with pink and painted the buildings rose. The water was pearl gray and very still. I sat on a low wall and stared out. It was incredibly beautiful, but I felt as if I were looking at a postcard. I hadn't realized until then how much I'd counted on a letter from Craig. Surely he'd have found time once during two weeks? Surely little planes flew the mail out, even if there was no post office? Horrible thoughts began to creep into my mind: Was Alaska an excuse to get away from me? Had he grown tired of me and wanted to break it to me gradually? I remembered how he had encouraged me to go to Europe—perhaps he wanted me to meet somebody new so that his own conscience would be clear when he broke up with me.

A steamer glided down the lake, leaving a silver trail behind it. I caught the faint sound of music across the water, and instantly I was back in Paris, standing with Carlo beside the Seine as the tourist boat passed. I could see his gentle dark eyes glowing as he looked down at me, and I could hear him saying, "Would you mind if I kissed you?"

"Are you deciding which mountaintop you want to sit on, to think?" Toni's voice cut into my thoughts.

"I was just thinking that they look rather cold," I said.

"And Venice would be much warmer?" she asked.

"Much warmer," I agreed.

Chapter Fifteen

"Do you realize that we're finally behaving like normal tourists?" Toni asked me. She was standing with her head out of the train window as we wound through the Swiss mountains. The air that blew in was fresh and crisp. Villages straight out of *Heidi* were nestled on the slope opposite, and waterfalls plunged down to the valley in a series of giant steps.

Toni turned back to look at me. Her hair was blowing every which way in the wind, and her eyes were shining. Now that she'd put the Philippe episode behind her, she was behaving like the old Toni again—energetic, bouncy, and "unsquashable." "Look at us," she went on. "We've done Lake Geneva—seen all the old castles and things—and now we're doing the grand train tour of Switzerland. Tomorrow we'll be in sunny Italy!" And she leaned out of the window again to wave at an old man riding along on top of a load of hay. The old man waved back.

Seeing Toni so relaxed and happy made me feel even more grouchy. "You'd better watch out for tunnels," I said. "I don't want your headless body to drop into my lap."

Toni looked down at me. "What's eating you?" she asked. "Are you upset that Craig hasn't written yet?"

"Of course not," I said hastily. "I mean, you know what film sets are like—busy all the time and no mailbox nearby and probably only one plane a week out to civilization—and all those wolves and polar bears and things. No wonder he hasn't written yet."

Tony sat down opposite me. "So you are worried," she said.

I looked out of the window and sighed. "I keep wondering if he's using this summer as a way to break up with me gently," I said. "After all, I've written to him several times already. I've thought about him. I wouldn't take Carlo's name and address because of him—"

"Is that why you've finally made up your mind to go to Venice—to spite Craig?"

"I don't know," I said. "I don't really want to spite Craig, but I don't want to spend my summer writing postcards and seeing castles if he's having a great time without me. Of course, I know that my chances of meeting Carlo again are one in a million. He probably doesn't ever go through the touristy parts of the city. I keep telling myself to be realistic—we'll go to Venice and see the Bridge of Sighs and St. Mark's Square, then we'll come home again."

That's what I kept telling myself, but every time I gazed out of the window, a little daydream crept into my mind, a daydream in which I was crossing a canal and there was Carlo, coming toward me and we'd run to each other and— stop! I said firmly. *This is becoming very dumb. You still love Craig, and you don't want to get involved with Carlo again. Understood?*

That evening we changed trains and caught the Venice express—a huge, rumbling giant of a train that had already come all the way through Europe. The train was crowded, but we managed to get a compartment with just one other person in it—a shabby old man with lots of white beard. He was asleep opposite us, clutching a black bag to his stomach as we came in. He awoke with a start as we closed the door behind us, stared at us, and clutched the bag even tighter. The train groaned its way out of the station and roared off into the dusk.

"This is very smart of us to pick a night train," Toni said. "It saves us a hotel bill."

"It's all right for you, you can sleep anywhere," I said. "I'll probably be awake all night."

Darkness fell. Toni fell asleep instantly, and I drifted into a half-dreaming state in which I imagined that Craig had sent me a polar bear in the mail. The bear tried to eat me, and I tried to escape from it by climbing onto the luggage rack.

I awoke as the compartment door opened. A small, thin man with a pencil-thin mustache put his head around the door and said something to the old man. The old man nodded and said something back. Then the thin man closed our door again, and we both drifted back to sleep.

The next time I woke, it was to feel someone shaking me. I opened my eyes, and it was still quite dark. "What's the matter?" I asked. "Have we got there yet?"

"Jill, something terrible's happened," Toni said urgently.

I opened my eyes fully. "What has?"

"The old man. He's gone."

I looked at the empty space opposite us. "I expect he's gone to the bathroom or maybe the dining car," I said.

"But he's been gone for hours."

"Then he got off," I said.

"But we haven't stopped anywhere," Toni said. "Jill—you've seen all the movies. Things happen to people in European trains. They kidnap scientists and take them to Russia, and they trade spies, and they murder people—"

"Oh, come on, Toni," I said, looking around uneasily. "Those are movies. In real life ordinary, boring people get on a train at one end and get off at the other. The man has gone for a walk, or he's standing in the corridor somewhere."

"Then walk up and down with me and see if we can find him!" she begged urgently.

The train was cold in the middle of the night, and I had no wish to go with her, but she was really upset. So we walked, from one end of the train to the other, without seeing him.

"There you are," she whispered. "Don't you agree now that he's been kidnapped? I bet he had secrets in that black bag. Remember how he clutched it all the time?"

"Well, anyway," I said, "I don't see what we can do about it, even if he has been kidnapped."

"Tell the conductor," Toni said urgently. "After all, the train hasn't stopped. He has to be on board somewhere. The conductor can have the train searched, and he'll be rescued."

"Oh, Toni," I said. "Why does everything you do turn out to be so complicated?"

We walked back through the train in silence. Then suddenly the train went around a curve, and we stumbled and grabbed at a handrail. The window blind in a compartment flapped open for a second, and in that second we saw—our old man sitting with the thin man with the mustache—the two of them alone in a compartment.

Toni clutched me again. "You see," she hissed. "What did I tell you? He's holding him prisoner. Now do you agree we should get the conductor?"

I didn't know what to believe anymore. I was feeling sick and scared. The swaying train with its flickering lights and rumbling wheels made the whole world seem unreal. I was almost inclined to believe Toni. "I guess so," I said hesitantly.

"Right," she said, rushing ahead of me down the train. Before I could even catch up with her, she grabbed the nearest person in uniform and poured out her story to him. By the time she finally made him understand, there was a good-sized crowd around us. They all insisted on following us back to the spy's compartment.

"I feel like a fool," I whispered to Toni. "I wish you hadn't ever started this."

"Just think how you'll feel when you save our old man and get your name in all the papers," she said proudly.

We reached the right cabin. "In there," Toni said. "The old man with the white beard. He's the one who's been kidnapped."

The conductor flung open the door. Two surprised faces looked up. Rapid conversation took place. The two men looked astonished, then angry, then they both started to laugh.

The conductor turned to us. "This man is a friend of the other. They meet on the train last night. This man invite other man to come and play chess in his compartment. You see, chess?"

We both looked and noticed, for the first time, the traveling chessboard between them. Our large crowd broke into noisy conversation, all talking and laughing loudly at once.

"I think the little Americana like the spy movie—no?" one man asked Toni, ruffling her hair.

Toni stalked ahead of me back to our own seats. She looked furious. Being made fun of was the worst thing in the world for her.

"Don't say it," she said through clenched teeth.

"I *will* say it," I said. "Next time you want to go and rescue someone, you can do it alone. I'm going back to sleep."

"Well, he might've been a kidnapped scientist," she said. "And the world might've been very grateful to me. Stupid old man. He shouldn't have clutched that bag or gone to play chess."

"And you should learn to act like a normal tourist," I said. "Now shut up. I want to get some sleep."

Toni went over to the window and lifted the blind. "Hey, you can't sleep now," she said. "Come and look at this."

"What is it?" I asked grouchily. "A spy signaling to the train? A helicopter chasing us?"

"No, dummy," she said impatiently. "It's Italy!"

I got to my feet and went over to the window. The world outside was still pearl gray. Gray fields stretched out before us. No more mountains. As we watched a thin golden line on the horizon, the sun rose above it like a ball of flame. Instantly the gray landscape turned Technicolor—brilliant hedges of red and purple flowers, purple grapes spilling over white porches, yellow church towers, green shutters, green fields full of ripe watermelons and tomatoes. As Toni lowered the window, we could hear a church bell ringing slowly and solemnly. The air that wafted in smelled rich and scented.

I stood staring out as if I were in a trance. Suddenly I felt all those layers of tension and worry slipping away. It didn't matter anymore that I hadn't slept most of the night. Nothing mattered anymore except that I was in a new and exciting country and I was going to have a wonderful time there.

Chapter Sixteen

Two hours later we were in Venice. The train had actually crossed to the island on a bridge, and we stepped down to brilliant sunlight and a rich, but not unpleasant, muddy, seaweedy smell. We left our bags at a small hotel near the station and just went exploring, wandering through narrow alleys and crossing canals by curved bridges.

"Hey, this place is fun," Toni said, leaning down over the Grand Canal and watching a procession of motor boats chugging up and down. Some boats carried fruit and vegetables. Others were water buses, and we watched passengers get on and off as if it were the most normal thing in the world. A mail boat went past and a boat full of chickens in cages. Someone leaned out of an upstairs window and yelled something at the man in the chicken boat. He laughed and yelled something back.

"You know what this reminds me of?" Toni asked as we walked on. "A very old Disneyland."

I laughed, but the more I thought about it, the more I had to agree.

"So what'll we see first?" Toni asked as we sat down for a midmorning cup of coffee in St. Mark's Square. "Personally I think the weather's much too nice for churches and museums. In fact, I'm very tempted to go to the beach for the day."

"That's not a bad idea," I said. "Let's go find out where the beach is."

We wandered down to the steps where lots of motor boats were moored. While Toni was asking about beaches, I let my eyes wander and saw something that caught my attention: "Half-Day Tour—Venice Glass Factories."

Toni tapped my arm. "He says we get a boat to the Lido from here. You want to go back to the hotel and find our bathing suits?"

"I've been thinking," I said. "I don't really feel in a beach sort of mood after all. What I'd really like to do is tour the glass factories."

"The what?" Toni asked, looking at me as if I were not right in the head.

"The glass factories—where they make all that lovely, curly glass."

"I never knew you were interested in factories

or glass," Toni said. "And I don't know if I'm really anxious to stand next to a furnace while someone blows hot sand in my face. I think the Lido would be much more appealing."

"Oh, but this is very special," I said. "You have to see it. It's world famous."

"Then it can go on being world famous without me," Toni said.

"OK. So I'll go alone," I said calmly. "I'll meet you this evening."

Toni looked at me very suspiciously. "You never like going anywhere alone," she said. "Why is this so special to you?"

"No reason," I said. "I'd just like to see glass made."

"Oh, well," Toni said with a sigh. "I suppose I'd better suffer with you. After all, I did drag you to Europe in the first place, and you were very nice about Philippe. If it means that much to you . . ."

So we climbed onto the boat, and soon we were chugging across the harbor to another small island. We saw three glass factories. In all of them, as Toni had predicted, we stood in the blazing heat and watched men twirl threads of liquid flame into magic flowers. It was very interesting, but not actually what you'd want to do on a hot afternoon. And in every factory while the guide was explaining things to us, I looked around carefully for anything that might remind me of Carlo. I stared at people in the gift shops and dared myself to ask if the owner's son was called Carlo, but I couldn't make myself say the words.

So when we chugged back to Venice late that afternoon, I was no nearer to finding him. I gazed out across the totally calm surface and tried to get my thoughts in order. I had realized all along that it was impossible, of course. You just don't find somebody in a big city. The glass factories we'd been to were the ones that tourists went to. There were probably hundreds more, hidden away where tourists would never find them, and Carlo was not likely to be in one either. He had said that he hated working there.

Maybe Toni's idea wasn't such a bad one. Maybe the next day we'd try the beach. After all, that's where any intelligent young Venetian would be on a hot day—if he'd returned to the city at all.

The sun was setting as we walked back across the city. It winked back at us from hundreds of windows as we went down the Grand Canal. Even the water was tinged with pink.

"Cheer up," Toni said as we began walking to the hotel. "How about we go out dancing to a nightclub?"

I sighed. "Toni, I've never been to a nightclub in my life, and I guess I'd be scared to go to one on my own. That's just my problem, I know—I was born conventional."

We came to the last bridge before our hotel, a

steep little bridge with steps up and down. I plodded up the steps ahead of Toni, still muttering. "I wish I could change the way I am, but I can't." I paused on top of the bridge to look back at the pink-tinged buildings, the lines of washing flapping in the evening breeze, and the pigeons circling above the rooftops. "It's all right for you," I went on. "You seem to go through life as if it's a big game. I'm not like you—I don't do crazy things. I live my proper little life, never doing anything unexpected or crazy or unusual."

I glanced down at the dark, oily water below us. A gondola was passing under the bridge. I looked at it, then looked again. Suddenly someone in the gondola was standing up and waving madly.

"Jeel!" he was yelling. "Jeel!"

"Carlo!" I screamed in amazement and stepped back, off the bridge and into the canal.

Chapter Seventeen

The next few minutes were total confusion. I heard Toni screaming from the bridge above, Carlo yelling my name from close by. I had heard enough rumors about the canal water to know that I didn't want to swallow any. I screwed up my eyes tightly and pushed my lips together as I fought my way back to the surface. I came up close to the gondola.

Carlo was still standing in the boat. "Jeel, don't worry. I will save you," he cried. I tried to tell him that I could swim perfectly well, but I was scared to open my mouth in case canal water got in. So before I could prevent him, Carlo had peeled off his light jacket and dived in beside me.

"Jeel," he cried, coming up next to me and

grabbing at me. "Don't worry. I have saved you."
His arms came around me, effectively preventing
me from swimming.

"It's OK, Carlo, I can sw—" I managed to say
before my head went under the water.

Luckily the gondolier had sense enough to get
his oar under both of us before Carlo succeeded
in drowning me. He propelled us to the steps,
where we climbed up, both panting like beached
whales. My mouth had the foul taste of canal
water in it, and mud and weeds were stuck to my
skin. Carlo was panting a lot harder than I was,
and it occurred to me that he wasn't the world's
greatest swimmer. That made his rescue all the
more touching.

"Are you OK?" I asked as he started coughing.

He looked up, and his whole face broke into
that wonderful smile. "Oh, Jeel," he said. "Is it
not enough that you drop the purse on my head?
Now you have to drop your whole self on my
head, too! A simple hello would have been
enough!"

"Oh, Carlo," I said, gazing at him and shaking
my head in disbelief. "Is it really true?"

"I cannot believe it either," he said. "When I
left you in Paris, I thought I would never see you
again. I thought you did not want to see me
again. I thought it was hopeless. You did not
have my name. You did not have my address. I
never dreamed—oh, Jeel, now do you believe it is
fate?"

"It must be," I said. "It really must be."

Then his arms came around me, and we sat there without speaking, my head on his shoulder as if it were the most natural thing in the world.

"Are you both OK?" Toni's voice interrupted. She squatted down beside us. "I wondered if you were giving mutual mouth to mouth?"

"Not yet," Carlo said, looking up at her with a little smile. "How nice to see you again, Tonee!"

"We always seem to meet in interesting circumstances," Toni said. "But you'll be amazed to hear that I had nothing to do with this one. In fact, I was just walking along beside my friend here, listening to her tell me how she never did anything unusual. Then she just turned around and stepped off the bridge!"

I started to laugh. The whole thing was so ridiculous. Life was so ridiculous. I'd been hoping and dreaming about meeting Carlo again. I had looked for him in all the places he should have been. Then I'd fallen on him. If that wasn't fate, what was? Suddenly I sneezed violently.

Toni looked alarmed. "We'd better get you back to the hotel quickly," she said. "You don't want to catch pneumonia or anything!"

"But you must come back to my house. It is not far," he said. "My mother will take care of everything."

"But she'll need clean clothes and things," Toni said.

"I have sisters," Carlo said. "She must be taken good care of. My mother will know . . ."

I sat there, listening to this conversation but taking no part in it. Actually I was not feeling too wonderful, and the thought of Carlo's mother taking care of me sounded pretty good. Carlo half carried me back to the gondola. He said something in rapid Italian to the gondolier, who helped me to the seat.

"Where is your hotel?" Carlo asked. "I will send our man for your clothes later. First she must have a bath and a hot drink."

We all squeezed into the seat with me in the middle.

"You don't look too great," Toni said. "Are you feeling all right?"

"I swallowed a lot of water," I said. "I don't feel too great."

I was shivering by the time we pulled up at some impressive steps. Carlo leaped out and ran in through a big carved doorway, telling us he'd be back immediately.

Immediately Toni turned to me. "You know this just isn't like you," she said. "All my life you've told me that I do dumb things because I don't think. And now you're going into a strange house—just like that!"

"But I know Carlo," I said.

"Hardly," she said. "Anyone can be charming

one day in Paris. After all, you know nothing about him. You'd never go to someone's house at home if you'd only met the person once."

"Then you don't think we should go?" I asked.

"I didn't say that," she said. "I'm sure Carlo is very nice and very respectable. I just wanted you to know that you can do dumb and impulsive things when your heart is ruling your head. It's nice to see you're just as bad as I am."

"Oh, Toni," I said. "It's like a miracle, isn't it—to see Carlo again. I never thought it'd happen."

"Even though you tried hard enough," she said, grinning. "Interested in glass blowing, my foot!"

I never got a chance to defend myself because a mob of people suddenly came rushing out of Carlo's house and pouring down the steps toward us. I don't know how many there actually were, but it looked like an invading army. There were old people and young, female and male, and they were all talking and yelling at once. Toni and I gave each other a scared look as a large man leaned down into the gondola and scooped me up with one movement. A small, birdlike woman bobbed along beside him, screaming instructions in a very unbirdlike voice. I lay quietly in the man's arms, too astonished and scared to do anything sensible like struggle, while I was carried in through the big, double doors. I got a fleeting impression of a gloomy marble hallway, then a shady courtyard, then steps going up and around, paintings on the ceilings and carvings on the walls until at last I was deposited on a couch in a cool, high-ceilinged room.

At this point Carlo appeared again beside me, with the little bird-woman who chattered at me breathlessly.

"It's no good, Mama," he said. "She does not speak Italian." He turned to me and smiled. "My mother thinks the whole world speaks Italian. Unfortunately she speaks no English, but she wishes to know if you would like her to call the doctor right away, if you would like a drink of hot tea or cool lemonade, if you would like a bath or merely to change into clean clothes?"

"Oh, I don't think I need a doctor, thank you," I said quickly, still overwhelmed by the people crowding at the doorway. "And I would like a bath and some hot tea, if that's OK?"

"Everything is OK for you, Jeel," he said, sitting down beside me and taking my hand. "When I think that you nearly drowned—"

I didn't like to tell him that I was probably a better swimmer than he was *and* that I had my senior lifesaving certificate. I merely smiled while Carlo conveyed my wishes to his mother, who in turn yelled instructions to the host of people at the door. Even though she was tiny, she was clearly the boss. People scurried off in all directions as she barked orders at them. In no time at all I was soaking off the revolting mud and slime in a huge hot bath, then sipping equally revolting herb tea as I lay back, dressed in a tentlike white nightgown in a room overlooking the canal.

All through the evening a succession of people wandered in and out. Since most of them spoke no English, it was hard to figure out who was a family member and who was a servant. I had no idea how many sisters Carlo had because all of the women appeared to look and dress exactly alike—a family of clones. They came in, smiled prettily, and then left again.

Toni didn't appear until it was almost dark, and I began to worry that they had not invited her in or allowed her to stay.

"Phew, what a business," she said, collapsing heavily onto the end of my bed. "How are you feeling?"

"Oh, I feel fine again now," I said. "I'm all clean and respectable, and they've taken away my clothes for washing. Where were you? I was getting worried about you."

"I've been back to the hotel to get our things," she said. "Carlo's mother insisted we come and stay here, so I went back with Carlo's brother and sister in the gondola. He's cute, by the way—Giovanni, Carlo's brother, I mean."

"I gather from that twinkle in your eye that you got on well together," I said.

She giggled. "Well, these Italian boys do have a

certain charm, don't they? Boy, Jill, we're having good luck now. Think of the great time we can have in Venice—boys to escort us to all the in places! So don't go catching double pneumonia, will you?"

As it happened, it wasn't double pneumonia I caught at all. I fell asleep, feeling contented and fine, then woke in the middle of the night to be suddenly and violently sick to my stomach. The doctor had to be called, after all, first thing the next morning.

He examined me and shook his head. "What foolishness is this?" he kept asking. "It is not advisable to drink the canal water. Bad water in canals cause much problems. Do you see Venice people drinking canal water? No, you do not."

"I didn't actually intend to drink it," I said. "I fell off a bridge, by mistake."

But that just made him "tut-tut" all the more.

"Now you must rest and not eat for several days," he said as he left. "Until we have chased away the bugs, no?"

The next few days were dreamlike, and not always filled with pleasant dreams either. I certainly didn't feel like eating and only made a half-hearted attempt to swallow a few spoonfuls of the broth or tea that Carlo's sisters brought up to me. I was so grateful that his family had taken me in. I could never have survived in a hotel room because some of the time I felt very, very ill. Toni even wanted to phone my parents a couple of times. Carlo looked very concerned and spent most of his time at my bedside. So we did a lot of talking and got to know each other in a way we'd never have done if I'd stayed healthy.

The more I learned about him, the more I liked him. He was so deep and thoughtful, as well as being funny at times. He tried to translate some of the poems he'd written into English, and even in translation I could tell they were good.

"But my father, he says 'bah' to such things," he said to Toni and me one evening. "My father says a real man works with his hands not his heart. I shall have to take over the factory one day because I am the eldest son. Giovanni, he is lucky because he does not have to work in glass factory. He can study to be a doctor as he wishes."

"Just tell your father that the factory isn't for you," Toni said.

Carlo laughed. "You do not yet know my father," he said.

"I know him," Toni answered. "And he seems like a big pussycat to me."

Carlo looked amazed. "My father—a pussycat?" he asked. "Are we talking of the same man?"

I tended to agree with Carlo. His father had struck me as a very frightening person—tall and big-boned with powerful arms and a perpetual scowl on his face. True, he had been in to see me several times and asked politely how I was feeling, but I wouldn't want to be on the wrong side of him.

"Oh, sure," Toni said. "He even laughed when I beat him at checkers last night. And he said he was flattered that I liked his company."

"Toni's having a wonderful time," I remarked to Carlo as she left.

He nodded. "She has fitted in perfectly well with my family. They all like her—even my father, so it would seem. And boyfriends—do all American girls pick up boys every time they go out?"

"That's just Toni," I said. "Most of them are like me—they have to wait to drop themselves on the right boy's head."

"And am I the right boy?" Carlo asked, suddenly serious. His hand inched forward to take mine. I felt the tingle go all the way up my arm.

"You're a very special boy," I said. For a long time we stared at each other without talking.

"Do you remember when we walked together beside the river in Paris?" he asked at last.

"How could I ever forget it?" I answered.

"I asked you then if I could kiss you—and you said no."

There was a pause.

"I thought I'd never see you again," I said. "And I didn't want to get involved."

"Do you still not want to get involved?" he asked in a low voice. His face was only inches from mine. His eyes were gazing at me seriously.

155

"I think I already am," I whispered as his lips came toward mine.

The kiss seemed to go on forever.

"Carlo," I said when at last we broke apart, "what if I'm still infectious!"

He laughed. "I'll take the risk," he said, kissing me again. "Besides," he continued as that kiss ended, "I am an old Venetian. There is nothing in this water that can harm me. The goddess of the sea watches over us and brings us good things. After all, she brought me you."

"It was hardly the goddess of the sea," I said, brushing back a dark curl from his forehead. "It was a dumb American girl stepping off a bridge."

"Oh, Jeel," he said, holding me close to him. "Now you must hurry and get strong quickly so that I can show you my city and we can ride in the gondola together and dance together under the stars. There is so much to do."

And not much time to do it, I thought, remembering that I had wasted precious days lying there sick.

"Now that I have found you again, I don't think I will ever let you go," he whispered, nuzzling my ear. Feeling his strong arms around me and his lips searching for mine, I wasn't at all sure that I ever wanted to go, either.

But the romantic scene was cut short by a screech from the doorway.

"Carlo!" his mother yelled, letting out a stream

of rapid Italian. Carlo grinned and moved apart from me.

"She says it is not proper and that your parents will never forgive her if I visit the young lady in her bedroom without a chaperon." He rose to his feet. "You know what this means, don't you?" he asked, his eyes teasing mine.

"That we'll have to have a chaperon in the future?" I asked.

"Are you crazy?" he asked, laughing down at me. "It means that you had better get strong and get up right away so that we can have some privacy where my mother can't spy on us."

He blew me a kiss as she closed the door firmly behind him.

Chapter Eighteen

The next week was full of perfect days spent with Carlo. His family owned a motorboat, and we went out in it together all the time, sometimes taking Toni and Giovanni with us to the Lido to swim, sometimes alone. Luckily Toni had more than enough to keep her busy. She and Giovanni hit it off really well, and you could often hear them roaring with laughter as they went through the house like hurricanes.

Toni made daily trips to the post office to see if we had any letters and usually came back with a letter from Rich. Also some from my parents. None, however, from Craig.

She also spent a lot of time with Carlo's father, playing checkers or arguing about anything. Carlo's father loved a good argument, and he and Toni had terrific shouting matches in which he thumped the table and turned purple in the face. Since Toni was still convinced he was a pussycat, she was not in the least scared by this. Carlo's father thought she was wonderful and even took her to his factory one day.

She came home very excited that evening, right after Carlo and I had arrived back.

"Boy, what a day," she said. flopping down flat on the marble floor. "It gets so hot in those glassblowing places."

Carlo nodded. "Now you understand why I do not wish to work there."

Toni raised her head. "Oh, it was interesting though. I tried blowing something, but it came out as a long squiggle." She laughed at the memory of it. "And do you know what your father said?" she asked, her eyes teasing Carlo. "He said he wished I was one of his children because then I could take over his factory one day, and I'd make a better job of it then either of his sons "

"Really?" Carlo asked. "And what did you say to that?"

She grinned. "I told him that he wasn't fair to you. I told him he had no right to force you to work in the factory when you didn't like it and you wanted to be a famous writer."

Carlo's eyes opened very wide. "And my father—he became very angry, no?"

"Strangely enough, he didn't," Toni said. "Tell me, Carlo. Have you ever actually discussed your future with your father—I mean, sat down together and talked about it?"

"There was nothing to talk about," Carlo said stiffly. "He expected me to take over the factory. That was that. He would not want to listen to my dreams."

"But that's where you're wrong, Carlo," Toni said. "Do you know, he had no idea you wanted to become a writer, and he didn't even know that you didn't like the factory. He was interested, and he said that you had an ancestor who was a famous poet once and that explained everything."

"He wasn't angry?" Carlo asked. "I do not believe it. I never dared to mention my dreams because I was so afraid of my father and his anger. So did he say I could become a writer?"

"He said you'd better go to college some more, and he didn't want you writing any of this modern stuff full of sex and violence."

Carlo leaped up. "But, Toni, that's marvelous," he said. "How can I ever thank you? You have changed my whole life."

Toni smiled serenely. "Oh, yes, I'm a regular fairy godmother," she said. "In fact, you owe a lot to me. After all, I was the one who knocked the purse out of Jill's hands in the first place. And I was the one who stayed home that evening so that you two could be alone together."

"Toni," I said suspiciously. "But you were sick that evening. . . ."

Toni shook her head solemnly. "Am I the sort

160

of person who ever gets sick?" she asked. "I could tell that you two had hit it off instantly, and I thought you needed more time alone."

"Toni Redmond," I growled. "What a nerve. Talk about a matchmaker. I should really—"

I got up and started dropping pillows on her, while she covered her face and giggled.

"Stop, stop," Carlo said, grabbing me and pinning my arms to my sides. "You cannot harm the person who got me out of the glass factory! I forbid it!"

"And, anyway," Toni asked from between the pillows, "aren't you glad I stayed home that night?"

"Aren't you?" Carlo asked, rubbing his cheek against mine.

"I guess so," I said calmly. "After all, I haven't had a bad time the last few days. A bit boring, maybe, but—" The rest of the sentence was never finished because Carlo started attacking me and his mother came in to see what all the noise was about.

One day stands out in my memory, the sort of day that I'd like to preserve in a glass bottle to take down from the shelf and look at over and over again. Carlo and I went alone in the boat to one of the other islands. The water in the lagoon was totally still, reflecting back buildings and trees like a sheet of glass.

At last Carlo turned off the engine, and we

moved with the tide, rocking gently as a larger ship passed us on its way out to the Mediterranean. I lay resting on the side of the boat, staring down into the brown water and trying to spot a fish. Carlo moved over to sit beside me.

"Jeel," he said, "I have been thinking. . . ."

I looked up. His hand caressed my shoulder and then my back.

"I have been thinking how perfect this has been. You and me. We have a wonderful time. We understand each other well. I almost lost you once, Jeel, and I do not want to let you go again. Why don't you stay?"

I really wasn't prepared for this. "But—but, Carlo," I stammered, fighting for the words. His closeness and the rocking boat confused me. "I have to get back."

"Why?" he asked.

"Because it's all planned, and I want to go to college and get on with my future."

"And if your future is not over there, Jeel? If it is here?"

"Carlo—we've only known each other two weeks. How can you talk like that?"

"But you have been happy these two weeks, have you not? And is not happiness the most important thing in life?"

"I guess so," I said, "but—"

"No buts," he said gently. "Can you not put off this college for a while? Maybe spend a year over here, and then you could judge what you wanted from life."

"Oh, Carlo," I said, staring down at the glittering water below. "I thought I knew what I wanted out of life. . . ."

"This boyfriend at home in America. You have not talked of him, but do you still think of him?"

"I thought about him all the time until last week," I said. "I thought he was the most important thing in my life, but he hasn't written to me once, and since I've been with you, I've hardly thought about him. So I don't know, Carlo, I'm really confused. I don't think I'm ready for any long-term plans yet."

"But would you not like to stay here longer with me? Are you not having a good time?"

"Oh, of course I am," I said. "I've had a wonderful time here, and I would like to stay longer."

"Then stay," he said, laughing; his eyes warm and full of joy. "Stay until you know me well enough to say, 'I like you more than the cowboy at home.' "

"But what if I decide I like the cowboy better?" I asked.

"Then I will cry a little and let you go," he said, shrugging his shoulders.

"Oh, Carlo," I said, reaching out to touch his cheek. "Why do things always have to be so complicated? Why can't I be like Toni—a different date every week and never a broken heart?"

"Because you feel things very deeply, Jeel, just

163

like I do," he said. "We belong together. Tell me that you will stay."

"I'll think about it, Carlo," I said. "That's all I can promise right now."

"And I shall do my best to convince you," he said, putting a finger under my chin and drawing my lips toward his.

"Carlo!" I said, pretending to be shocked. "There is no chaperon, remember!"

"We have all of Venice harbor for chaperons," he said. "See—a ship passes over there, and I am sure the sailors all approve of what I am going to do now." Then he kissed me in earnest, a kiss that went on forever and ever. I didn't even know or care if ships full of people were passing us.

When we finally set off for home, the sky had turned a dull gray.

"I think a storm will come," Carlo said. "Can you not feel it in the air?" He put the engine into high gear, and we shot across the glassy surface.

By the time we reached the shore, the clouds were hanging low and heavy over the city. It was so humid that everything felt clammy to touch. Mosquitoes hummed annoyingly as we tied up the boat and climbed the steps into the house. I went straight up to the bedroom I shared with Toni and found that she was still out. Walking over to the window I leaned against the cool marble of the windowsill and stared out across the rooftops and canals. I heard the first growl of thunder from far off and watched as the first plump raindrops spattered onto the hot tiles below me. I hadn't realized until then how much I missed the rain.

I was still leaning out watching as Toni came in.

"Hey," she said. "Didn't your mother ever tell you about leaning out of windows in thunderstorms?"

I looked around and smiled. "With all these church spires around, I don't think I really have too much to worry about," I said.

"We were so lucky," Toni said, flinging her purse down on her bed. "Another five minutes and we'd have been soaked to the skin. Boy, isn't it sticky today? What were you staring at so hard when I came in?"

"Me? Oh, nothing special. I was just thinking."

"About what?"

"Nothing special."

"About you and Carlo?"

"All right, Miss Nosy. About me and Carlo."

"Did he ask you to stay on?"

"Were you out there spying in the lagoon?"

She laughed. "Didn't you see my snorkel behind the boat?" She came and sat down on my bed. "No, actually, Jill, Giovanni told me that Carlo didn't want you to go. He says that Carlo's never been this involved with a girl before. Usually he's the playboy of the family and has a different girlfriend every week. So what did you tell him?"

"About what?"

"About staying on, dummy."

"I said I'd think about it, Toni," I said with a sigh. Sometimes she could be a pest. This was something I really wasn't ready to discuss right then.

"Really?" she asked, interested. "You'd really think about staying on here?"

"Well," I said slowly, "I am having a good time—"

"And what about Craig?" she asked. "Have you given up on him?"

"I should say it's more like he's given up on me. I mean, not one letter in four weeks. Doesn't that tell you something?"

Toni leaned over and retrieved her purse. "I went to the post office today," she said, rummaging inside. "I got two letters from Rich. You got another one from your parents—and this." Then she handed me the letter, redirected from Seattle. I could see from the original postmark, it had taken over two weeks to get here.

"Oh," I said.

Toni got up. "I'll leave you in peace for a bit," she said. "I bet Angelina needs help getting in the wash before it's soaked." Then she went, closing the door behind her and leaving me to stare down at Craig's letter.

I had longed for this ever since we arrived i

Europe. Now I was afraid to open it. I just sat there staring at it for a long while before I could make myself rip it open.

"My darling," it began.

I've no idea when this will reach you, as we're totally cut off from civilization and you'll be flitting around Europe. But I hope it catches up with you somewhere soon. I hope you're having a wonderful time, seeing a lot of new things, and having new, exciting experiences. I can just imagine you sitting in the hot sun outside a sidewalk café, watching the people going past and wondering whether to swim or see another museum after lunch. You don't know how I'm envying you or how I long to be beside you. I hope you spare a minute every now and then to think about me up here. Right now it's eleven at night, still not totally dark as the sun hardly sets this far north. It was really hot all day, and they had us dressed in fur suits. I thought I was going to melt away. Now at night it's suddenly cold. A wind is whipping down straight from the north slope, and I can hardly hold the pen in my hand.

Most of us go straight to sleep after work because we're so tired and bored. I lie awake and think about you looking elegant in Paris. I don't think I ever knew what lonely was until now. The other extras and I have nothing in common. They aren't in college and think I'm dumb to waste my life studying when I could be in "movie biz" full-time! (After this experience, I'd rather dig graves or be a sanitation man than be in movies.)

Outside, the storm had moved in. A clash of thunder made me jump and the letter almost slid out of my hands. The rain started coming down in earnest, drumming like applause on the roof above me. I was reminded of another freak rainstorm, when Craig and I had gone out for the first time and had nearly been washed away together. I remembered how he had rescued me from stampeding spectators at the concert and dragged me to shelter and told me I was beautiful even though the rain had destroyed my hair and washed away my makeup—I smiled as I read the rest of the letter.

Jill, I keep a calendar on my wall, and I cross off the days until I see you again. I keep wishing, very selfishly, that I hadn't let you go to Europe without me. I keep worrying, in the middle of the night, when the wind whips through this ten-man tent, that you'll meet someone else. Still, I suppose people think dumb things in the middle of the night, don't they? By daylight I tell myself that you've really written to me and

your letters are all sitting in a sack somewhere waiting to be delivered!

If you haven't written yet, please write. I
miss you so much. Did I mention that
before? And I can't wait until August when
we are both back home. There, it's mid-
night. I can cross off another day. I love you,
Jill.

Craig

P.S. We all drove ten miles yesterday
across the bumpy tundra, just to look at a
polar bear. Doesn't that show you how des-
perate we're getting?

It was much later when Toni came back into
the room. "Are you still here?" she asked. "Big
drama downstairs. The courtyard's all flooded.
Maria's having hysterics. Why are you sitting in
the dark?"

"Just thinking," I said, sighing loudly.

"Was it—I mean, what did Craig say?" she
asked.

"How much he missed me. How he crossed off
every day until we could be together again," I
said and swallowed hard.

"Then why hadn't he written before?" Toni
demanded. "It's all very well to miss someone
after you've put that someone through four
weeks of worrying!"

"This has taken two weeks to get here," I said.

"He hadn't received any of my letters, either. He thought I'd given up on him."

"Oh, Jill," Toni said. "And what are you going to do now? What about Carlo?"

I shook my head slowly. "It's no use, Toni. I knew it as soon as I read that letter. If Craig had said come to Alaska instantly, walk the last hundred miles across the ice, I'd have done it. I guess all this with Carlo, I was trying to tell myself that I didn't really need Craig, that it wouldn't matter to me if we were through. Carlo just happened to be here."

"That's not what he thinks about you—that you just happened to be here."

"I know. That's what's going to make it so hard. Thank heavens this letter arrived when it did, Toni. There must be a sort of magic spell about this place. You know, I was really seriously thinking about staying here. It even crossed my mind to marry Carlo! I must have been crazy!"

"But Carlo's a very nice person," Toni said. "He's good-looking and he's fun and he's smart—"

"Oh, I know," I said. "He's all of those things. And I really like him—well, more than like him— but we don't belong here, do we? I was thinking how good the rain felt this evening. I never thought that I'd miss the rain, but I do. And this house with all these people . . . Don't you sometimes long for something familiar? Our living room at home and 'Loveboat' on TV and peanut butter and jelly—"

"And a tall glass of milk!" Toni said.

"And a shower that works!"

"And phone calls and hamburgers and even my brothers," Toni yelled.

We stood there looking at each other.

"Oh, Toni," I said. "Let's go home."

Chapter Nineteen

I didn't sleep much that night. I lay awake listening to the noises floating up through my open window—a shout, a burst of song, a baby crying, the put-put of a small motorboat—city noises without the honk and rumble of traffic. And as I lay awake I tried to think what I was going to say to Carlo in the morning. Because the big problem was that I had lied to Toni and even to myself a little. Carlo wasn't just somebody who happened to be around to make me forget about Craig. He was somebody very special. I'd known that from the first moment I met him. In fact, I was in love with him, if it was possible to be in love with two boys at the same time.

The only problem was that I loved Craig better. With Craig I was secure and comfortable. We were like old married people, as Toni had said. He no longer made my heart skip a beat every time he called me. With Carlo I was living all the excitement of a new love, and it had been wonderful. But now it had to end. I was sensible enough to see that. I knew all too clearly that I did not belong here. It was a fun place to visit, but I missed my home. In the morning I would have to tell him that I was leaving, and I didn't know how to do that without hurting both of us.

He appeared when I was in the middle of breakfast. We ate breakfast in the courtyard, in the shade of a huge purple bougainvillea that dropped butterflylike flowers onto the tablecloth. Behind me the house was full of noise. Maria, the cook, was still complaining about something—I could hear her shrill voice coming from the kitchen. Angelina, Carlo's sister, was singing as she dusted in a room above. The radio was going in Giovanni's room, and two other sisters were fighting. The normal level of noise for this house was loud and vital. But that morning it no longer felt exciting. I thought of breakfast at home—my father would've already departed for his office, my mother would hum softly as she watered her plants. Otherwise warm, comfortable silence as I ate.

"*Ciao*, Jeel," Carlo called, bounding out. "It is a beautiful morning. The city has been washed clean and new in the storm. Everything sparkles and steams. A good day for walking. Hurry and eat and we can go."

I hated to see him in such a happy mood when I had such bad news for him. I felt mean as I walked beside him out into the early morning air. We walked together in silence through the alleyways, Carlo striding out at a great pace and breaking every now and then into a loud snatch of song. Underfoot there were puddles, and the flowers in their dusty corners had all woken up, renewed and bright. In St. Mark's Square the café owners were sweeping the puddles away, while the pigeons rose into the air with a sound like wet clothes flapping on a line every time there was a gust of wind.

"Come," Carlo said, dragging me forward. "Today we climb the Campanile—the bell tower. Today is so clear. The view will be worthwhile."

We climbed and climbed, going round and round inside the narrow tower until at last the city lay below us, rooftops steaming as if they were alive and breathing.

"It's a good thing this is you and not Toni," Carlo said with a chuckle. Think of the damage she could do with a purse dropped from this height!"

I smiled as I looked out over the lagoon to the islands we'd seen together.

"Jeel," he said in a much softer voice. "Something is wrong, no?"

I looked up at him, at those dark, gentle eyes that seemed to glow.

"You are so quiet today," he said. "You have not said a word, I think. You have much on your mind, no?"

"Yes, Carlo," I said slowly. "I have much on my mind."

"Would you like to tell me about it?"

"I'm not quite sure how to, Carlo. That's the problem."

"I think I know what it is," he said softly. "You want to say you are leaving me. But you do not wish to hurt me—"

"How did you know?" I asked, gazing at him.

"I read it in your eyes, Jeel. Your eyes tell me that you miss your home. I was a fool to have asked you to stay yesterday. It made you weigh the difference between Venice and home, and all the things you missed most came floating to the surface. I am stupid. If I had said nothing, maybe you could have stayed here long enough so that I meant more to you than any—"

I reached out and touched his arm. "It wasn't just you, Carlo. I got a letter from Craig yesterday—the first one I've had all summer. I realized how much I've missed him, too."

"I see," he said, staring out past me to the islands. "So he is the one you love after all." There was a long pause. "I really thought—" he said at last. "I really thought that this time it was right. For both of us. When fate brings me the same girl twice, how can it be wrong? I thought you felt as strongly about me."

"I do, Carlo," I said. "That's just the problem. I really am in love with you. But I've always been good old sensible, levelheaded Jill. Not like Toni. Toni dragged me to Europe to chase after a boy. I'd never do a thing like that." I could feel myself starting to cry. I looked out, away from him so that he wouldn't see the tears. "I just know that it would be wrong for me to stay here. I'd never feel at home."

"And if I came to America, chasing you?" he asked. "Because I am like Toni. I would do crazy things for a girl I loved."

"No, Carlo," I said. "That wouldn't work either. Don't you see—part of the reason I fell in love with you was because you were exciting and different and part of this exciting and different country. In America you'd soon feel lost and homesick. The sun hardly shines where I live. We have a long winter and lots of rain, and people cannot walk down the streets singing. And houses are locked up and quiet. You belong here, just as I belong at home."

"So you will go home and forget all about me," he said quietly. I turned toward him, and his eyes, too, were full of tears.

"Oh, no, Carlo," I said. "I will never forget all about you. Don't you understand—saying goodbye is just as hard for me. I'll remember you all my life. You'll probably be the one exciting thing that ever happened to me—and when I'm a housewife with my two point one kids and a dog and a station wagon and I'm a Brownie leader and a Little League mother, I'll think back to Venice, and I'll wonder what might have happened to my life if I'd dared to stay here."

"Then dare to stay," he begged, grabbing my arms fiercely and turning me toward him. "I don't want to be the one exciting thing in a whole boring life—"

"But it's no use, Carlo," I said as the tears rolled freely down my cheeks. "I can't change the type of person I am—and the type of person I am has to go home where I belong. Even if it's stupid and I'll regret it for the rest of my life."

"I really loved you, Jeel," he said. "I have said that to many girls in my life, but this is the first time it comes straight from my heart." He turned and walked ahead of me, down the echoing stairway.

Down in the square I caught up with him. "What will you do now?" I asked. "Will you go back to the university in Paris?"

"I don't think I will ever go back to Paris," he said. "I think I will write my first novel, now that I have suffered. They say that you must suffer if you want to write well, don't they?" He turned and gave me a little smile. I reached out and took his hand. He squeezed it and gave me a wonderful smile. "Don't worry about me, Jeel. We Italians love to make much emotion out of everything. Soon I will be singing again as I walk.

Come, the cafés are open. We will have a capuccino together."

Carlo's family were all sorry to see us go. They hugged us and showered us with so many presents, including beautiful glass paperweights and beads from his father, that even *my* suitcase would hardly close. Carlo gave me a lovely soft leather purse.

"You see how soft it is," he said. "I do not want the next poor boy you drop it near to suffer."

I managed to smile, since we were in a roomful of people. "I don't think I'll be dropping any more purses," I said. "I don't think I can stand the consequences."

Then the whole family piled into a water taxi to take us to the station. They were all shouting and laughing and crying. Only Carlo and I said nothing. They found us corner seats in the express and wouldn't let anyone else in our compartment. Toni had one last argument with Carlo's father over whether trains were more comfortable than airplanes, and I noticed that she'd picked up a lot of Italian. I listened in amazement as she said goodbye to Carlo's sisters and mother. The same Toni who'd struggled through two years of French without managing to put together a single sentence. Now she not only spoke a language, but she waved her arms around like any true Italian.

Only Carlo was not waving and yelling. He took

my hands. "Goodbye, Jeel," he said. "This time I do not say *arrivederci* because I do not think that fate will be kind enough to bring you back to me a third time. But I will always hope—who knows. The future is very big and very wide. Who can say where our paths will lead us—but if they do not lead us together, I wish you much happiness with your cowboy."

"Carlo," I said, "for the last time, he's not a cowboy."

Carlo grinned. "At least I made you smile. I have been trying to do that all morning! This is how I want to remember you, with that little dimple in your cheek, smiling at me."

The train whistle sounded. Everyone scrambled out in a hurry. Doors slammed. Brakes sighed. Toni and I leaned out of the window. The train lurched forward and began to move. Carlo leaped up and kissed me one last time until his family pulled him back down. Slowly we drew away from each other until he was just a waving blur. And all the time I smiled so that he would remember me the way he wanted to. The train moved out into the sunshine and across the bridge back to the mainland.

"We're on our way home," Toni said. "Back to cold milk and showers and peanut butter sandwiches—back to American boys who don't go around pinching bottoms and telling me I am a beautiful girl. I can't wait. I've had a taste of European men, and I've decided I like Americans better. Maybe it's chauvinistic of me, but it's the way I really feel. You'll be seeing Craig, and I have Rich waiting for me. Did I tell you he's just bought a car, so I can drive to college with him—" She stopped and looked at my face for the first time.

"I'm sorry, Jill," she said. "I never realized. You really care about leaving him, don't you?"

I nodded.

"And he wasn't just someone to take your mind off Craig, was he?"

I shook my head.

There was a pause.

"Do you think you'll ever see him again?"

I shook my head again.

"Have you decided not to talk anymore?" she asked. "Because I want you to know that I've just spent the last two weeks learning Italian. I do not intend to learn sign language just to communicate with you."

"Oh, Toni," I said, laughing in spite of myself. "It hurts so much. I don't dare talk in case I cry."

"Go ahead and cry, then," she said. "You'll feel better if you do. After all, you've already seen me cry on this trip. I don't want you to get home being one up on me."

Tears started trickling down my cheeks as if a great dam had broken. "I can't believe that I'll never see him again," I said. "I can't believe that I could fall in love with someone that quickly, but I did, Toni. I really, truly loved him, and he was a wonderful person, but it would never have worked, would it?"

"I don't think so," Toni said, serious for her. She put an arm around my shoulder. "I just don't see you in a black dress cooking mounds of spaghetti for a houseful of people."

"I know," I said, laughing and crying at the same time. "I know I didn't belong there and I couldn't be happy there, but Carlo was so wonderful. I'm so confused, Toni. I still love Craig, but he never made me feel the way I felt sometimes with Carlo—as if I could reach out and touch the moon. I'll never forget him."

"Of course you shouldn't forget him," Toni said. "Everyone should have one special romance in their lives that they can look back on and remember when they are old and gray. Here, now it's my turn to offer you tissues, only you look like you could use more than I have!"

"Thanks," I said, wiping my eyes and blowing furiously. "You really are a good friend, Toni."

"I should have thought I was your worst enemy," Toni said. "After all, I got you into all this. I was the one who dragged you to Europe. I was the one who knocked down your purse and who schemed to get Carlo and you together. I've brought you nothing but trouble since second grade. You'd better stay away from me in the future."

"Oh, Toni," I said, shaking my head. "You're my best friend." Then she laughed and hugged me, and I could tell from the wet patch on my shoulder that she was crying, too. "I have to stick with you," I said. "Who else would keep you from walking under taxis and getting yourself into impossible situations?"

"At least I don't fall into canals!" she said, laughing. "And you said you were the one nothing happens to. I've had a terrific summer, Jill, and it's only been terrific because you were there to share it with me—and I'm sorry it had to end this way for you."

"Toni," I said, "I wouldn't have missed a single minute of it for anything in the world."

I stared out of the window. The train was speeding through fields toward mountains that were already rising to the north. We had a long trip ahead of us, but we were going home.

ABOUT THE AUTHOR

An experienced world traveler, JANET QUIN-HARKIN has lived in England, Austria, Germany, Australia, and the United States. She now lives in California with her three teenage daughters and a son.

PUT YOURSELF IN THE PICTURE!

Enter the SWEET DREAMS® Cover Girl Contest and see yourself on the cover of a SWEET DREAMS book!

If you've ever dreamed of becoming a model and seeing *your* face gazing from the covers of books all across America, this is the contest for you!

Girls from age 11 to 16 are eligible. Just fill out the coupon below and send it in, along with two photographs of yourself (one close-up and one full length standing pose)* and an essay telling why you enjoy SWEET DREAMS books. The Grand Prize Winner will be chosen by an expert panel of judges—including a beauty editor from *Young Miss* magazine!

The Grand Prize is a trip to New York City for you and your chaperone, where you will be photographed for the cover of an upcoming SWEET DREAMS novel! The Grand Prize Winner will also receive a complete professional makeover, have an interview at a top modeling agency and enjoy a dinner date with a SWEET DREAMS author!

Five lucky Second Prize Winners will receive make-up kits!

So don't delay—enter the contest today!

*Photographs must have been taken within 6 months of contest entry.

SWEET DREAMS Cover Girl Contest
Bantam Books, Inc.
Dept. NP
666 Fifth Avenue
New York, NY 10103

Name_____ Age_____

Address_____

City _____ State _____ Zip _____

No purchase necessary. All entries must be received no later than December 31, 1985. The winners will be announced and notified by January 31, 1986. Chances of winning depend on number of entrants.

Exp. 12/31/85

C17—9/85

☐ 25143	**POWER PLAY #4**	$2.50
☐ 25043	**ALL NIGHT LONG #5**	$2.50
☐ 25105	**DANGEROUS LOVE #6**	$2.50
☐ 25106	**DEAR SISTER #7**	$2.50
☐ 25092	**HEARTBREAKER #8**	$2.50
☐ 25026	**RACING HEARTS #9**	$2.50
☐ 25016	**WRONG KIND OF GIRL #10**	$2.50
☐ 25046	**TOO GOOD TO BE TRUE #11**	$2.50
☐ 25035	**WHEN LOVE DIES #12**	$2.50
☐ 24524	**KIDNAPPED #13**	$2.25
☐ 24531	**DECEPTIONS #14**	$2.50
☐ 24582	**PROMISES #15**	$2.50
☐ 24672	**RAGS TO RICHES #16**	$2.50
☐ 24723	**LOVE LETTERS #17**	$2.50
☐ 24825	**HEAD OVER HEELS #18**	$2.50
☐ 24893	**SHOWDOWN #19**	$2.50
☐ 24947	**CRASH LANDING! #20**	$2.50
☐ 24994	**RUNAWAY #21**	$2.50
☐ 25133	**TOO MUCH IN LOVE #22**	$2.50

Prices and availability subject to change without notice.

Buy them at your local bookstore or use this handy coupon for ordering: